Believing In Horses, Too

Believing In Horses, Too

Valerie Ormond

Printed in the United States of America

Library of Congress Control Number: 2014942898
ISBN 978-0-9736330-4-7

This is a work of fiction. All characters and events are imaginary. Their resemblance, if any, to real life counterparts is
entirely coincidental.

*Dedicated to military veterans, volunteers,
and Mom*

Contents

1

Help

A year ago, Sadie believed everything happened for a reason, and now she struggled for sensible reasons for anything. Surrounded by pictures of her family, artifacts from the many places she'd lived, and a jewelry box of treasured memories, she still felt alone in the dark. Even her special collection of porcelain horses on her dresser could not fill the emptiness she felt tonight.

As part of her ritual in her twelfth year, she prayed every night for her dad's safe return. But tonight, she also prayed for herself.

"Dear God," she called in silence. "Please look after Dad in Afghanistan. I know you do — but I thought asking for extra help couldn't hurt. Please bring him home to us happy, healthy, and soon. I should be praying for others, but I realize I need help, too. I'm obsessing over Dad.

"No matter how hard I try to think positive

thoughts, bad ones creep in there. I can't forget the loud noises I heard in the background, and how Dad pretended it was nothing. I can't help but notice he writes less and doesn't say a lot. It's been so long; I miss him so much, and I'm tired of being brave. Please keep my daddy safe. And if you have time, afterwards, please help guide me, too.

"Thank you for listening. Amen."

Sadie sobbed into her pillow so no one would hear, angry she couldn't control her emotions. Her sixteen-year-old brother, Austin, seemed fine, and Mom carried on as if Dad left for work up the road at a grocery store or something. Sadie hated asking for help and didn't want to worry anyone by showing her true angst. So tonight she asked for help, in secret, from someone who wouldn't discuss her problems. She hoped tomorrow would be a better day, and someone would send her answers.

Sadie controlled her flood of tears and tried to let reason take over. Prayer meant faith, and faith kept people strong. She needed faith. Sadie wanted to stop living in the past, as she had been. She needed to live in the here and now, even if it meant facing the present and the future she feared. She needed to face reality: What if something bad happened to Dad?

Every person and every single thing around Sadie changed, and she stagnated. Mom started an exciting new job. And even though Mom's job was all secretive, her enthusiasm radiated adventure. Austin found true love with his first girlfriend, Katie. Even Sadie's horse, Lucky, discovered a love interest at the barn, the stunning chestnut mare he made eyes at and whinnied to any time she came close. Dad fought for his country in Afghanistan, never complaining a day. Every life held a purpose — except

Sadie's.

Sadie had been thinking about it a long time. During the first six months of Dad's deployment, she committed to saving ten horses on their way to an auction. She saved their lives, and accomplished her goal. But now, her only goal was to see her dad return home safe. How sad — a goal she could not control.

Sadie felt so isolated. She couldn't share or communicate her worry with her family. And living in a community with no other military people, no one else would understand. So she lived a life of constant secret fear which grew every day. She needed a distraction.

When Sadie rescued the horses, she fell into the problem. It found her. She didn't want to volunteer again so soon for something as difficult. And besides, she still had follow-up work with the rescue horses. But that wasn't a big enough distraction.

Sadie looked at the photographs on the nightstand next to her bed. A moonbeam snuck between the wooden blinds illuminating her favorite photo of herself, Lucky, and Dad, bringing light into the darkness. Her Irish storytelling Grandma Collins would have called it a "sign," but she had no idea what it meant.

Sadie drifted off to sleep without recognizing that she had found the answer to her special prayer.

2

A New Day

"Cold enough for you?" the instructor asked, when Sadie entered the indoor riding arena early the next morning.

"It's never too cold to ride! Besides, Lucky likes the cold. See how happy he looks?"

"Yes, but horses can be rambunctious in this weather. Keep that in mind," her no-nonsense instructor warned.

Loftmar Stables hired Amanda Takacs two months ago. Amanda competed in riding since kindergarten and graduated from Virginia Intermont University, one of the best-known local equine studies schools. She had more ribbons, trophies, and titles than anyone Sadie knew, except for the barn owner, Miss Jan. Sadie missed her former instructor at first, but soon found each instructor brings something new. Amanda had instilled in Sadie a yearning to compete.

"Are you ready for your first group lesson with Lucky?"

"Yes, and I'll show you. I know Lucky, and he likes to be around other horses so much that I know he'll behave."

"And you're a good enough rider to control him. It will be good practice for him to be with other horses. And I know you'll still be riding in your private lessons with Miss Kristy plus riding on your own. It's good to give a horse some different experiences."

"I think both of us need practice riding in groups, and what better place to start than here?" Sadie flashed a smile, as her teacher moved along to help another student adjust her stirrups.

Turning to the assembled group, Amanda bellowed, "Okay, we have five riders in here today, so let's make sure we give everyone space. Remember your steering, and pay attention to what's in front of you. Be extra careful around Lucky, since it's his first group lesson. I know you are good riders, or I wouldn't have a young, inexperienced horse in here with this many of you. But keep your heads in the game." Although five feet tall, Amanda taught with the voice of a giant.

The five riders spaced themselves out walking their horses around the ring to the left when Amanda called, "Let's pick up a rising trot. Whoa — slow down, Becky, nice and easy — we're just warming up. Eyes up, Jimmy, and push your heels down. Eva, shoulders back, and slow down your posting. Sadie, bring that inside shoulder back and *push* Lucky into that corner with your inside leg. Nice job, Alex, way to keep that pony marching."

Sadie concentrated so hard. She never wanted to

be the one causing an incident in the arena. Especially not with the four-year-old colt she'd only been riding for five months.

Amanda interrupted her thoughts. "You're doing well, Sadie, and Lucky's doing fine in here with these horses so far. Now that *he's* going well, let's work on *you*. Lower your hands and puuusshhh down in those heels. Your leg is moving way too much. You're not squeezing enough with your calf."

Amanda was right. Sadie corrected herself. She just went from being the proudest rider to the most embarrassed. Lucky performed well; Sadie needed work. Think, think, think, and make all those body parts do what they are supposed to do.

As the lesson continued, Sadie felt better when she paid attention and realized everyone else made riding mistakes, too. Sadie considered the barn her home away from home. She'd boarded Lucky at Loftmar since she got him in August, and knew almost everyone here. She wondered if the others took the criticism so seriously, and her quick scan of the group told her "no." They seemed happy in the moment, warm in the cold, breathing and getting in tune with their mounts. A male voice behind her made her heart jump.

"Hey, hotshot, looking pretty good with that young horse in here with all the old guys." Jimmy trotted his quarter horse, Billy, to Sadie's left and cut the corner to get ahead of her.

"Thanks," she managed. Brilliant. Jimmy boarded at Loftmar, and was one of Sadie's first friends here. Sadie didn't have a boyfriend yet, and didn't want one. But for some reason, Jimmy made her feel like she wanted one. Sadie saw many of her friends turn into absolute dopes as soon as they had boyfriends, and she wanted to avoid that as long as possible. But Jimmy — cute, likes horses, funny, oh, and sixteen — never mind. Back to class.

"Keep tracking left, and prepare to canter...all canter," Amanda commanded.

Amanda's prediction regarding the horses' excitement level came true now. The horses and ponies raced around the ring, as riders cut through the middle, turned corners tighter, and maneuvered to keep from running over each other.

"Alex, slow down, half-halt that pony with your outside rein — don't just pull on his face. He's getting annoyed. Talk to him, say whooooaaa, eeeassy, and sit back," Amanda instructed, while Alex careened around the ring on Stuffy, the energetic black and white pony creating a small wind gust. Stuffy stood the size of a Great Dane dog and raced around like one, too.

Sadie sat deep and forced her heels down, and kept her hands low. She breathed in deep and remembered the hours and hours she practiced this with Lucky to prepare him for this moment. She thought *easy, easy, boy*, but didn't have to make major corrections during the canter. Horse and rider in sync, Sadie smiled and let the rhythmic movement take her far away. She believed in Lucky, and he was making her look good. Lucky was taking care of her.

They completed their lesson doing what Lucky liked best — jumping. The riders began over a series of trot poles spaced four feet apart on the ground to give riders a feeling for pacing and position.

As Sadie pushed Lucky through the paces, she heard Amanda say, "See, watch Sadie over the trot poles — stay steady and balanced like that." Sadie burst with pride and felt herself and Lucky again as partners, on the right track together. As long as Sadie paid attention.

After a few warm-up jumps, Amanda designed a jump course and built on it two more times adding more jump fences to increase the difficulty. She coached each student through his or her course and let each know how to improve the next go round.

Sadie watched her fellow student, Becky, navigate the large gray horse, Thor, over jumps and around turns like a professional. Sadie felt like a proud mom, since Thor was one of the horses she had rescued. Miss Jan adopted Thor for Loftmar Stables believing his age, breeding, and disposition would make him a good school horse. As with most things, Miss Jan had been right. Thor was an excellent lesson horse, and he demonstrated that talent now.

As proud as Sadie was of Thor, she still wanted to show the class how well Lucky could do. When it was her turn to go, she concentrated on her jump course keeping her heels down, eyes up, and body in the correct position. She remembered to breathe out over the jumps and to control Lucky's canter pace. She brought Lucky deep into his corners and headed him straight toward the jumps and straight after the jumps. Lucky was a natural athlete, but he needed human direction, too.

"That was beautiful! This is the kind of riding we want to see all the time. Lucky did great in his first group lesson. Your hard work is paying off, Sadie," Amanda said loud enough for the entire class to hear.

"Thanks," Sadie managed, reaching down to pat her horse's neck and watching a happy tear fall on her riding glove.

Grooming Lucky after their ride, Sadie gave him a huge hug and said, "We're going to make Dad so proud of us when he comes home. We're going to be beautiful," - and it dawned on her - "at the *shows*!"

Amanda had been trying to convince Sadie to compete in horse shows with Lucky since she arrived to teach at the barn. But Sadie had been afraid, unsure of her own ability to compete on an inexperienced or "green" horse, as they called it in horse lingo. But now Sadie realized this was something that would keep her focused, and be good for her horse, too. And as the timing looked now, Sadie could show her dad as soon as he came home from the war how much she learned, progressed, and grew in the year he'd been gone.

Sadie found the distraction she needed.

She decided she was going to do it; she was going to compete in the largest horse show series in the state, the Maryland Horse Show. She would show her young horse Lucky for the first time at the Prince George's Equestrian Center this summer. Sadie's decision wasn't saving lives and didn't involve romance, but it gave her an important goal, and one she could control. Sadie committed to doing the best she could.

"I believe, I believe, I believe," Sadie chanted softly, sharing her personal mantra between girl and horse. Lucky's pinto markings amazingly spelled out the words "I believe" in an abstract fashion. Sadie traced her horse's unique markings with her finger and remembered how those words always helped her see things right. Today was no exception. Lucky nuzzled Sadie's shoulder in what she interpreted as his surefire agreement with her latest plan.

Sadie sought out Amanda who was preparing for the next riding class.

"Amanda, I have some big news."

"Really? What?"

"I've decided I want to take Lucky to the Maryland Horse Show this summer," Sadie announced.

"That's great news! You know I've wanted you to do this. And I hope you want me to coach you."

"Of course I do! I don't know what to do."

"Don't worry, Coach Amanda will take care of you. And Lucky will shine. I'm so happy for you. We have lots of work to do, but it will be fun. What a big step for you."

Walking home from the barn, feeling as if she was walking on a cloud, Sadie thought back to her mood last night. She realized her focus on her horse and her riding chased worry from her thoughts. She concluded today was already a better day.

Sadie rushed in the back door stopping only to take off her muddy riding boots. She headed straight for the family laptop computer and sent an e-mail to her dad revealing her big news.

Within minutes, she double-clicked on the e-mail she waited for. Dad was obviously awake.

> From: Dad
> To: Sadie
> Subj: Re: Guess What?
> Wow! Can't wait to see you in the big show! I know you'll do great. What made you decide to do this?
> Love you, mija,
> Dad

Sadie thought for a minute before responding.

From: Sadie
To: Dad
Subj: Re: Guess What?
    I thought it would be a good idea. Gotta go
now, more horse stuff! Thanks!
    Love xoxo,
    Your mija

Sadie figured her dad must be excited, since he called her one of his special names. "Mija" was short for "mi hija" or "my daughter" in Spanish. Sadie and her dad shared many special bonds, and one was their pride in their Mexican heritage. Dad taught Sadie some Spanish words and used them at the best times.

And Dad's mija hadn't lied to him: she *did* think it was a good idea. Sadie just hoped Dad didn't reply with more questions about why she decided to do something today that she thought was a bad idea the past few months.

And now Sadie knew she couldn't back out of her decision. Her war veteran dad, Lieutenant Commander Navarro, couldn't wait to see his daughter compete in the big show.

3

Checking On Horses

"Time to go, Sadie," Austin reminded, tapping his watch and nodding toward the front door. Sometimes her brother reminded Sadie so much of Dad it was eerie.

"I know, I just want to look — well, you know — right. These people are treating me like a celebrity and everything. I can't go walking in there with my hair springing out everywhere." Sadie looked into the mirror and plastered down stray hairs escaping her ponytail.

"They won't care about your hair, but they will care if you are late." Geez, there was Dad again.

"Okay, okay, I'm coming." She turned to her brother. "What do you think?"

"The paparazzi will be disappointed your hair isn't all springy," he said in all seriousness.

They both laughed, and Sadie appreciated having a brother who made stressful times better. She considered talking to him about her current concerns, well, obsession, over Dad's safety. But Austin seemed so happy-go-lucky. No good reason to ruin his life, too.

"Bye, Mom!" Sadie shouted on her way out the door.

"Wait! I have something for you to take to the people at Maryland Therapeutic Riding," Mom said. "Since it's January, I couldn't pick fresh flowers from the garden, but here's a small basket of jams I made from last summer's fruit. They're not for the horses, but for the volunteers," she smiled.

"Thanks, Mom," Sadie said, grateful for her mom's thoughtfulness. "Now, I'd better go, because you-know-who is tapping his foot." Sadie started out the door in a hurry, but turned back.

"I love you, Mom," she said, and kissed her on the cheek.

"Love you, too, sweetheart — now continue to make us proud!"

Not long after Sadie and her Navy family moved to Maryland last year, Sadie saved ten unwanted horses from an auction, where they most likely faced bad futures, including possibly being turned into horsemeat. She succeeded in what seemed an impossible task for a twelve-year-old, to find good homes for all ten. She vowed to check on each of the horses in their new homes. Today she would visit one of the rescued horses, Goliath, at the Maryland Therapeutic Riding Center in Crownsville, Maryland, not far from her home.

Sadie's brother, Austin, drove Sadie around during much of her horse-saving crusade. And although Austin didn't like to admit it, he had been a large part of Sadie's success. Austin liked to stay in the background, almost like a stagehand. But he always appeared with the right props at the right time or had the right cue for the star. Sadie adored her brother and couldn't understand why so many other people complained about their brothers and sisters.

Sadie and Austin grew up in a military family, which meant lots of moves. When they arrived at new duty stations, they were on their own until they made new friends. Although four years older, Austin never treated Sadie like a kid, but he could be a tad protective. They shared a wonderful bond, and he exemplified Sadie's definition of a team player.

"So what's on the agenda today?" Austin asked, while keeping eyes on the road.

"We're supposed to meet with Mrs. Nayden, the development director. She's going to show us around and tell us what they do. We'll get to see Goliath again, and then we go home."

"I can handle that. If that's all we're doing, how come you didn't want Katie to come along?"

Aarrggh, Katie. Why did he have to ruin what started off as a good day?

"She just doesn't belong here. She has nothing to do with my horses, and she'd probably ask stupid questions. Besides, this isn't a spectator sport," Sadie quipped.

"Wow — that doesn't sound like you — not nice at all. And Katie's not stupid, she's my girlfriend, remember?"

"Sorry, I guess I'm just a little nervous about all this, and I don't really know what to expect."

"That's no reason to pick on Katie."

Her brother was so blind when it came to Katie, or "Katie-bug" as he liked to call her. So annoying. Katie, the little track star who even got Austin to join a school team for the first time ever. Perfect Katie, five-foot-three, 101 pounds, shiny straight long blonde hair and big round brown eyes with eyelashes as long as Lucky's. Heads turned wherever Katie-bug walked, but what she had in looks, she lacked in smarts. She repeated everything Austin said, and she never uttered an original thought. At least not that Sadie had heard.

"Earth to Sadie," Austin interrupted.

"Huh, oh, what's up?"

"Do you have a speech or anything that you want to practice on the way — kind of like the other times when you've brought me to these horse things that I don't know anything about?"

"No. Now I just get to look around, and if necessary, ask how the horse is doing. I remind them if the horse isn't going to work out to tell me so I can find another home. Mrs. Heritage from Freedom Hill Horse Rescue told me follow-up is one of the most important parts of horse rescue. Oftentimes when people find homes on their own, they end up being bad homes."

"Like what?"

"Here's a great example. You know about Pikachu, don't you?"

"Not really, Sadie, I really only know about *your* horses, which by the way, are not *your* horses anymore."

"I know, it's just that after thinking about them for so many months, I find it hard to consider them as anyone else's. And besides, they are still *my* horses to look after and make sure they stay in good homes. It's why we're on our way here today. But anyhow, back to Pikachu."

"Then please, tell me about Peekaboo," he said, making a right-hand turn.

"It's Pika*chu*, but we call her Pia at the barn. Remember how I said Freedom Hill keeps track of their horses after they adopt them out? Well, Freedom Hill rescued Pia from the same auction where we rescued the ten horses, but they rescued her a year before we rescued ours. They found her a loving home. And why not? Pia's an adorable chunky red roan mare with a wide white blaze on her face and matching white socks on her two back legs. Anyway, one day Freedom Hill gets a call from someone saying Pia's picture is on the website for horses saved from the meat buyers at the auction. Mrs. Heritage freaks, and checks out the picture, luckily to find out that it wasn't Pia."

"I'm not following you."

"That's because I'm not finished. So, because of this, Freedom Hill volunteers started checking the weekly photos of the horses saved from auction. They wanted to make sure something like this didn't happen for real to any of the other horses they saved. And guess what happened?"

"Peekaboo showed up."

"Yes! A few weeks after the wrong Pia-sighting, she shows up on the website, and Freedom Hill went back to the place holding her and re-adopted her. Isn't that amazing?"

"Sad is more like it. What did the people say who adopted her from Freedom Hill and sent her to the meat buyers at the auction?"

"They didn't know she went to auction. They couldn't afford her anymore and let someone take her who said he would give her a good home. They felt terrible, but that doesn't change the fact that Pia could have been sold for meat because those people didn't check to see what happened to her after they gave her away."

"Where is she now?"

"*That's* the best part of the story! She's at Loftmar Stables with Lucky, Thor, and the other happy horses. Miss Jan became real interested in Freedom Hill when we first saved the horses and ended up being a foster mom for several rescue horses."

"I remember you telling me that now; I just don't remember you telling me this whole story."

"Well, there's a time and a place for everything, right?"

"Anyhow, Miss Jan found homes for two of the other horses, but Pia took to Loftmar so well, Miss Jan decided to adopt her. So now Pia gets attention every day, and lots of people love her. She's such a good girl. It's hard to believe what almost happened to her — twice."

"Now I understand why it's so important to keep track of *your* horses. Great story, and check it out, good timing. We're here."

4

Maryland Therapeutic Riding

Austin turned right at the Maryland Therapeutic Riding sign, driving up a long driveway lined with rolling pastures and pristine white fences. Even in winter, the fields remained green, and grazing horses spotted the landscape.

"Drive to the end and park in front of the office sign," Sadie ordered, in charge.

"Yes, ma'am," Austin replied.

Sadie's heart thumped and she took a deep breath to relax. Since she'd become involved in this whole horse-saving ordeal, she kept finding herself in situations that seemed so adult. Here she was meeting with one of the directors of this major organization. She wished now that she had taken up her mom's offer to go with her. But it was too late.

"Here," Austin said, handing Sadie the basket with the homemade jams and pickled vegetables Mom prepared. "Remember to tell the lady these are for the humans, because the horses may not know how to open the jars."

Sadie laughed, shaking off her self-doubts, and said, "Let's go get 'em."

Austin opened the office door for Sadie and gestured with a flourish for her to enter. He put her at ease. Sadie smiled and gave him a look that said, *"Be on your best behavior now, funny brother."*

"Can we help you?" a young woman asked, who was seated at the first desk, decked out in muddy barn clothes displaying a day's hard work.

"Hi, and yes, thank you. I'm Sadie Navarro, and this is my brother Austin. We're here to meet Mrs. Nayden."

An adult voice from the back room rang out. "Sadie, I'll be right there." Seconds later a tall thin woman with a perfect blonde bob hairdo wearing a Navy blue business suit emerged. Sadie now appreciated the extra thirty seconds she spent fixing her hair this morning. Mrs. Nayden reminded Sadie of the local news reporter, Diana McGlade, as she had that same welcoming smile and electric demeanor. Sadie felt better already.

"It's such a pleasure to meet you, little superstar," Mrs. Nayden began. Mom told Sadie it was rude to argue with people when they complimented you, so Sadie gritted her teeth and tried not to show her embarrassment. She never bargained for superstar status when she decided to save the horses.

"I'm Marilyn Nayden, development director for Maryland Therapeutic Riding. Rather than sit in here and talk, how about we take a walk around and I can tell you all about our history, and show you our facilities?"

"And your horses," Sadie chimed in.

"Of course, our horses — especially Goliath."

Sadie handed Mrs. Nayden the basket, thanking her for taking the time for the visit. She gave her brother a sideways glance, wondering if he would mention the intended recipients of the gifts. But Austin simply smiled and held open the door while the three departed the office. Mrs. Nayden began her smooth description of Maryland Therapeutic Riding as their feet crunched on the semi-frozen ground.

"Many people aren't aware that the founder began the program because she, herself, found healing through horses following a tragic automobile accident when she was a teenager. She wanted to bring this same freedom and healing to others, and so began the effort in 1996. Today, we offer many tailored programs and serve over 200 people a year, all at no cost to the participants. We're very fortunate to have many generous sponsors, and of course we couldn't operate without our army of volunteers."

Mrs. Nayden showed them the orderly tack room, the handicapped-accessible bathroom and shower, and the mostly empty barns because the majority of the horses were busy grazing in pastures or participating in lessons. Sadie found it fascinating, but also felt a little impatient. She wanted to scream: "I'm here to see Goliath!" Pushing Goliath to the back of her thoughts, she tried to concentrate instead on every detail of the tour.

"Since you both are from a military family, you might be very interested to know that we have a Maryland Therapeutic Riding Horses for Heroes program in which we treat wounded veterans."

Sadie almost choked. Yes, she remembered seeing it on their website, but that was before she'd had the recent secret "Dad thoughts."

"We have a special treat for you today," Mrs. Nayden continued. "You're going to get to see Goliath at work!"

"With who?" Sadie asked, biting the inside of her cheek.

"With one of our students, Joey, who has been with us for many years. Goliath has turned out to be a perfect fit for him now that he is bigger than he used to be. You will be amazed to see them together. Joey has autism, and we, and other therapeutic riding centers, work with autistic students with great results. Research proves the rhythm and balance activities open up learning receptors in the brain and help release hormones that make people feel good. You will see."

Sadie's pulse slowed realizing she would not be watching a wounded veteran right now. She couldn't help but imagine at any moment that could be her dad. She still couldn't speak. Austin eyed her, and rescued her from her speechlessness.

"That will be great. Come on, Sadie, remember how long it's been since we've seen Goliath? Last time we saw him, he really needed a bath, and at least a few hundred bales of hay."

5

Miracle Worker

Mrs. Nayden entered the spacious wooden indoor arena first, followed by her guests.

"Look!" Sadie gasped, eyes tearing and smiling a full-toothed grin, pointing at the giant palomino Belgian draft horse standing stoically at the mounting block. The sight of Goliath overrode all earlier emotions.

"Wow, he sure looks different," Austin said.

"Can we go see him?" Sadie asked, restraining herself from running over and hugging his enormous leg, remembering the last time she touched with him three months ago at the livestock auction.

"Sure, let's go. Let me introduce you to everyone."

Sadie tried to tamp down her emotions. But the memories flooded back to her first encounter with Goliath, knowing she had to help him, losing him to another bidder, and then regaining him. Sadie's eyes were moist, and she used the length of the arena to get herself back under control. Austin just followed along as if all this was nothing.

"Jennifer, and Mrs. King, I'd like you to meet Sadie Navarro, and her brother, Austin. I told you about them — the horse savers — and that they would be here today," Mrs. Nayden reported, elevating them to celebrity status.

"And this is Joey," she continued, introducing the young rider who had just mounted Goliath. "And of course you know Goliath."

"Nice to meet you all," Sadie nodded, and moved to Goliath's shoulder. As she moved to pat his gigantic neck, Goliath turned and nudged his head in her direction, releasing a knowing nicker.

"He remembers you," Austin said, with both eyes and mouth smiling.

Sadie nuzzled against him stroking his sparkling clean winter coat feeling the silkiness of his mane. This was a far cry from the mangy, filthy, but proud horse she'd seen not that long ago, whose owners had abandoned him like a worn-out car. Sadie realized she had an audience, and embarrassed, looked up, to take in Joey patiently watching her.

"I like him, too," he said, and shared a smile saying more than words.

"I'm sorry; I didn't mean to interrupt your lesson. It's just..." Sadie stopped.

"It's okay, he's happy. You can pet him," came the small voice from the boy willing to share the horse he only got to ride for a half hour a week.

Jennifer, the instructor, suggested, "All right, Mrs. Nayden, I've got them from here, if you'd like."

"Thanks, Jennifer, I'll head back up to the office then. There's always work to be done. Don't be strangers, now, kids, and if there's anything we can do, please get in touch," Mrs. Nayden said, waving goodbye.

"Sadie and Austin, why don't you stand over here with Mrs. King, and let me work with Joey. We'll show you what we can do. Goliath is a saint, and will stand here forever if we ask him to. But he wants to show off for you a little, I think."

Jennifer led Goliath and Joey across the arena, leaving the small group behind them.

"I'm so happy to meet you, Sadie," Mrs. King started. "I can't tell you how much Goliath has meant to Joey. He is such a special horse, so gentle, and he seems to understand Joey so well. It's a miracle."

"Well, thank you, and it's nice to meet you, too. And I'm happy Goliath and Joey met, too," Sadie chuckled, to keep from crying.

"When they told me a twelve-year-old girl had saved this horse, I didn't believe it. That just wasn't possible. I read all the news articles the center posted about you and Goliath, and I have to say that you are an incredible inspiration to people."

Sadie hated this part. At some point it had to stop. She didn't want to seem disrespectful to people who were trying to be nice. But she felt awkward when people praised her for doing something she had to do at the time.

"It wasn't just me," Sadie answered. "My brother helped me tons, and a whole bunch of other people, like my mom, my teacher, my school friends, a state delegate, *Capital News*, horse rescues, and many, many more. I'm from a military family, and I've been taught that things get done best as a team, right, Austin?"

"Hmm? Oh, yeah, right." Austin stood mesmerized by Jennifer, Goliath, and Joey walking and performing a series of circles and halts in the arena. "Check this out, Sadie — watch them. It's like Goliath knows what Joey is thinking or something. And I swear that horse is smiling."

"I'm not a doctor," Mrs. King continued, "but I can talk from my research, and from being Joey's mom. I've known him before beginning equine therapy and since coming here for five years now — since Joey was ten. Besides the repetitive rocking motion and warmth of the horse that helps autistic people communicate, there's something else very special about horses."

"Please, tell me...I understand horses are special, but I don't understand the connection with autism," Sadie said, always inquisitive, and listening while observing the ongoing lesson.

"It's like the two beings recognize something familiar in one another. There are so many stories where autistic children approach horses or ponies for the first time, and the animals submit to them, dropping their head, trusting them, almost listening. I rode horses for many years, and I know that is not normal."

"No, it's not," Sadie said, recalling normal horse-human interactions.

"Someone put it this way: there are strong similarities in the way horses and those with autism see the world. Horses are often born into an environment they don't understand, with overwhelming sights, sounds, and smells, and a sense that no one understands them. And when they see someone with autism, who has much the same background, and who knows them, and knows what they need — there is a connection. Since the two share the same experiences, they both relax, and seem to *talk* and understand each other," Mrs. King said.

"That's fascinating," Sadie said, looking back to the horse and rider pair, visualizing what Mrs. King described.

"When I first brought Joey here, he didn't speak. And you heard him. And he doesn't even know you. If you'd like to learn more about autism, remember the name Dr. Temple Grandin. She has autism, and has written and spoken extensively on the subject, including the connection between animals and autism."

"Thank you, I will remember that. I really would like to learn more," Sadie said, repeating the name to herself so she wouldn't forget.

Jennifer called from the middle of the ring. "Sadie, would you like to come over here and participate?"

"Go ahead," Mrs. King encouraged, "you'll get more out of seeing than from listening to me."

"I don't know. You just shared an awful lot with me. It makes me want to work with horses and therapy when I grow up," Sadie announced, as she strode to the center of the arena. "Come on, Austin, she meant you, too."

"Yes, boss," he said, following.

As the three reassembled in the middle of the arena, Jennifer instructed, "Sadie and Austin, I want you two to stay here. We're going to show you a pattern Joey and Goliath have practiced. It was Joey's idea, to show you how much he appreciates you bringing Goliath to Maryland Therapeutic Riding. Are you ready, Joey?"

He nodded, and Sadie noted his concentration as he began to walk away from them on the diagonal heading toward the corner. Jennifer walked beside them, speaking quietly, but the control was Joey's, and Goliath's. The draft horse stood 16.3 hands, or 5 feet 7 inches, at his withers, below the mane, even taller than Lucky. Goliath's head made him even taller, and he held it high right now, as if he comprehended he was performing. The massive steps rocked Joey in the saddle side to side, and although slow, he covered a lot of ground with each step. Joey giggled, followed by Goliath's nicker. A horse giggle?

Toward the end of the diagonal, Joey pulled the right rein and turned his right hip, shoulder, and head to signal to his mount to bend right. They maintained course on a small semicircle for about ten steps, and then executed a perfect halt at a 45-degree angle in the center of the ring. Sadie started to clap, but Jennifer shook her head, meaning it wasn't over yet.

Joey's shoulders rose in a deep breath, and lowered again. Facing Sadie and Austin, Joey pivoted Goliath, pointing him the opposite direction toward the other corner. Goliath plodded off in another half-circle away from them, and Joey maneuvered him back to the right in a diagonal line opposite of the one he'd traveled the first time. Jennifer whispered something to Joey which made him relax and laugh. In five more mammoth steps, the team halted in front of Sadie and Austin.

Sadie decided to hold her clapping this time, in case they weren't finished. She concentrated on the pattern they had traveled and understood.

"That was a heart, from Joey and Goliath," Jennifer said. "It took a lot of practice, but these two never gave up."

Now Sadie clapped. Joey patted Goliath's neck, saying thank you.

"What a great demonstration, Joey!" Sadie exclaimed.

"Put it here, partner," Austin said, extending a

high-five.

That was it. Sadie couldn't hold the tears anymore. And she didn't think she had to. Joey looked at her, puzzled.

"No, no, — I'm so happy — and I don't know how to show it."

"You can pet Goliath again," he offered.

"Thank you," Sadie said, and buried her wet face in Goliath's clean blond mane, as he dropped his head to her. "Thank you, all."

Sadie regained her composure and stood up, with her tall shoulders back. She lifted her right hand to her forehead in a salute and said, "Goliath, I always knew you were a good soldier. We're all very proud of you." She dropped her salute and hugged his chest and the top of his enormous leg, feeling his warmth and slow, steady breathing.

Sadie and Austin bid their farewells, and Maryland Therapeutic Riding invited them back anytime they wanted to visit. It had been an emotional day, but Sadie gained such joy from knowing the gentle giant Goliath found his special purpose in his life.

6

New Kid on the Block

An old man lived in the house next-door to the Navarros, on the hill behind a rickety chain-link fence. Sadie met Mr. Brogan when her family first moved to Bowie, but he never said much. Sadie thought how lonely he must be, by himself, but also saw how much time he spent in his gardens. Like Sadie's mom, Mr. Brogan enjoyed gardening, so at least his plants, flowers, vegetables, and trees kept him company. Sadie always smiled and waved when she passed him on her way to the barn and wished the poor soul had more to life.

Sadie got her wish when little Brady Brogan ambled into her yard and knocked on the front door. It had to be a stranger knocking, because anyone familiar used the back door when visiting. Opening the door with the chain on, Sadie met her gentleman caller through the crack.

"Hi, I'm Brady Brogan, your new next-door neighbor. Would you like to come out and play? And do any other kids live near here?" asked the enthusiastic curly-haired blond boy.

"Sure, I'll come out." Sadie hollered upstairs, "Aauusstiinn, I'm going outside — believe it or not, there's someone new in the neighborhood!" She grabbed her coat and met her visitor on the front porch she never used.

"Hmmm…you make a new neighbor sound unusual. I've lived in lots of places, and we've always had people moving in and out," Brady said.

"Well, so have I," Sadie replied, indignant, as if this kid was implying she was a country bumpkin who had never moved. "But this isn't exactly a neighborhood — it's kind of in the sticks — and no one has moved in since we've lived here for six months."

"That's weird. Well then, I'm glad to meet you, and I'm sure we'll have great adventures together."

This kid talks like something out of an old movie, Sadie thought.

"To answer your other question, no, no other kids live near here. My brother, Austin, is sixteen, so he's not a kid. He's great, and you'll like him. Everyone does. His latest thing is running. He never wanted to play team sports until Katie Sitarski convinced him to run cross-country. Now he runs after Katie," Sadie laughed.

"Do you have a boyfriend?"

Kind of nosy kid. "No, not yet. But I have a special guy in my life. Want to meet him?"

"Umm…I'm not sure. Will he be jealous?"

"I don't think so. But we can find out. Are you allowed to walk back to the barn?"

"What barn?"

"Geez, you're so worldly and have lived all over, and you don't even know there's a horse stable behind your house?" Sadie regretted saying it as soon as the snide words came out.

Brady's enthusiasm drained from his face. His lips turned down, and he stared at his hands. "No, I don't know anything about this place except my step mom kicked us out again and Dad said the only place we had left to go was to live with Grandpa. We came all the way from Colorado in our car, and got here yesterday. So, no, I didn't know about a barn. You're the first person I've spoken to here except my grandpa, who I didn't even know, and who didn't know we were coming."

Way to go, Sadie.

"I'm sorry. If it makes you feel better, I've moved around a lot, too." *Hadn't she just said that?* "I wasn't happy about being here at first either, but it got way better. Just like it will for you."

"Do you think so?" he asked, looking up to her.

"Of course I do, or I wouldn't say so. Are you allowed to take a walk? It's safe."

"Sure, I am. I have *free rein*, as my dad says. It means he's not around much to tell me what I can and can't do. And Grandpa's not used to having a kid around either. It's why he sent me over to say hi to you. He said you were always very nice to him and had a cheerful aura."

Sadie doubted Mr. Brogan chose those exact words, but she was pleased with Brady's interpretation. And at least Brady seemed to be over the zinger she stung him with just moments ago.

"We're off, then, for our first great Brady-Sadie adventure," Sadie said, and linked his arm in hers, which surprised him. She let go, realizing he didn't appear to have been brought up the same way she was in a touchy-feely family.

Brady chattered on the way to the stables, and asked Sadie at least fifty questions during the five-minute walk. Sadie thought of the huge change for Grandpa Brogan shifting from dead quiet to Mr. Inquisitor. She discovered more about this bundle of energy beside her in their first ten minutes of friendship than she knew about her school friends she had known for months. His strong personality defied his weak appearance.

"How old are you, Brady?"

"I'm ten and a half," he answered, sticking out his chin. "How about you?"

Sadie hid her surprise; she thought he was seven or eight. "I'm twelve...and a half. My birthday is in June."

"Lots of birthday shopping time." He smiled, and then frowned. "If we're still here by then."

"I hope so," Sadie said, feeling sad for his uncertainty. "But let's talk about *now*. Are you ready to meet my special guy?" Sadie asked.

"I think so," Brady hesitated.

Sadie and Brady entered the barn and stood in front of Lucky's stall. Lucky, always curious, poked his head over the stall door and stretched out as far as he could to nuzzle Sadie, who reached forward and scratched him under his jaw. Lucky showed he liked it by stretching his neck out even farther, asking for more.

"Lucky, meet Brady. Brady, meet my special guy, Lucky." Sadie smiled, continuing to stroke her personable horse.

Brady stood still. "I've never touched a horse."

"Well then, it's time. Come on, I told you it would be a great Brady-Sadie adventure! Lucky won't hurt you."

Brady reached toward the pinto's muzzle while

Sadie scratched behind her horse's long brown ears tipped with a line of black hair. Brady jumped when Lucky lifted his head, as if nodding, telling him it was okay to touch. Brady took a deep breath and tried again, this time connecting, touching the hair on the side of Lucky's face. Stroking the horse's nose, Brady looked into his giant expressive brown eyes. Lucky stared back at him, ears perked forward, appreciating his new fan.

"He's the most amazing animal I've ever seen — and now, touched," the boy cooed. He beamed while enjoying Lucky's reaction to his pets, and Sadie knew she had created another horse lover.

"And just think, you live right next to Loftmar so you can visit here all the time! Come on, I'll teach you how to groom," Sadie said, jostling Lucky's forelock. She was happy to have made Brady's day.

Sadie grabbed Lucky's tack box with all her grooming tools and set it outside his stall. To be safe, she put a halter and lead rope on her horse before bringing Brady into the stall. She showed Brady each brush one by one and explained its purpose. Sadie noticed the boy's fascination with how she picked the dirt out of Lucky's hooves.

"Wanna try?" Sadie asked, holding out the hoof pick.

"I d-d-don't know how."

"Of course you don't, but I'll teach you. Come on over here." Sadie waved him to her side and explained step by step what she was doing. "Why don't you try this last front hoof? And don't worry, I'll help."

Brady positioned himself in the right place and leaned into Lucky, who picked up his hoof like a gentleman. Sadie saw Brady squinting in concentration as he followed her precise instructions. He looked up to Sadie for approval, and a second later Lucky turned his nose and bumped Brady's behind.

"You're done," Sadie laughed. "Even Lucky approves."

Brady placed Lucky's foot back down, smiled, and turned to pat Lucky's nose. The boy who had been afraid to touch him not long ago was now comfortable in the stall with this giant horse.

The two toured the barn, and Sadie introduced her new pal to the humans and the horses. Sadie made sure to point out Nessa, Lucky's love interest. Brady concluded handsome Lucky chose well with the lovely, graceful, feminine chestnut-colored mare. Amazed by it all, Brady took it in. Sadie could tell he only asked half the questions he wanted to ask.

When she thought she saturated him with enough newness for the day, she said, "Let's go. We'll come back again. I promise."

Brady nodded, and Sadie could tell he didn't want to leave. "Thank you, I'd like that very much." After the first 100 steps of the 200 steps back home, Brady spoke again. "Sadie, my grandpa doesn't say much, and he doesn't know me at all. But he saw I was sad when I got here. I don't think he knew you much, either, but I'm sure glad he sent me in your direction."

"I'm glad he did, too, Brady. Don't be a stranger. You are always welcome — and that's my parents' rule, too. We've grown up in different places and understand what it's like to be alone. Thank you for coming over. And since you're living here, we'll see each other a lot."

"Do you think we'll go to the same school?"

"Yes, and I'll even save you a seat on the bus and

34

show you around."

"Thank you, Sadie. It's nice to have a friend. I'd better go, but I look forward to our next adventure." Sadie observed the small boy traipsing up the hill to his grandfather's house and thought about the things he said. A step mom who threw him out, a dad who didn't care what he did, traveling across country in a car, and staying with a relative he had never met. And yet this child was so kind and full of love, and now Sadie's mysterious new friend.

7

New Beginnings - A New Job

"Hi, Miss Kristy," Sadie said, as she entered the indoor arena leading Lucky for her afternoon riding lesson. On Tuesdays, Sadie took lessons with Miss Kristy Alvarez who taught at Loftmar one day a week, helped with summer camps, and hosted a horse club at the stables. Sadie loved her tough lessons with Amanda, but she also enjoyed her more laid-back private lessons. Each instructor taught different techniques.

"What's wrong? It looks like you and Lucky don't have any pep today," Miss Kristy said, checking the buckles on Lucky's bridle.

"You are right. At least about me."

"And you know Lucky feels that, too. So what's going on?"

"Well, since you asked, I was all excited because I found out I wanted to be a horse therapist," Sadie proclaimed, as she mounted her 16.1 hand horse with ease, realizing how much easier it got as she kept getting taller every day.

"How great! How did you decide this?" Miss Kristy asked, while eyeing Sadie's tack ensuring everything was in the right place. "Go ahead and start by tracking left. Let Lucky walk and stretch out some. Loosen up the reins a little and let him drop his head — there you go, that's good."

"Do you remember that one of the horses we saved went to the Maryland Therapeutic Riding Center?"

"Uh-huh. Eyes forward. And bend his body more in your corners. Step in your outside stirrup, and bring your inside shoulder back a hair. There you go."

"Sorry, I guess I don't talk and ride so well at the same time."

"Yes you do, keep going. It's my job to try to help you be better. I won't interrupt you for a whole lap now, I promise. Think about what I said. Concentrate on those four elements. Go ahead with your story," Miss Kristy coaxed.

"The people at the Maryland Therapeutic Riding Center invited me to visit Goliath and to see what they do there. It's amazing! They have all these programs helping different kinds of people. I got to observe Goliath doing his job, and it was one of the neatest things I've ever seen. So, I decided I wanted to do equine therapy when I grow up," she said, still concentrating on her riding position.

"That's wonderful, Sadie, and I'm sure you will be good at it. You have a good way with horses and people — a perfect combination for therapy work. But I guess I don't understand why this makes you sad."

"Well, I figured I could volunteer, and get started now." Sadie didn't finish the sentence with the rest of her thought — because she needed the distraction now.

Sadie breathed out hard, and stopped Lucky in his tracks without being asked to do so. She looked directly at Miss Kristy. "But when I checked Maryland Therapeutic Riding's website, I found out I couldn't volunteer there until I'm fourteen. That's over a year away."

"Really? That's a long time."

"You don't even know how long that seems to me," Sadie said, urging Lucky forward into a walk, hoping somehow he would make her feel better.

"Well, I may have good news. You could volunteer with me and get experience. Besides working here, I run my own organization which uses horses to help people. We focus on using rescue horses in our work, and you already understand more about rescues than most people. But let's talk after your lesson. Right now, you need to ride, and Lucky looks like he's getting tired of all our small talk."

Miss Kristy put Sadie and Lucky through the paces, walk, trot, and canter in both directions. After the warm-up, Sadie soared over a course of jumps, more exhilarated than usual. She loved jumping Lucky. She felt the two of them become one when he lifted himself in the air at the right spot, with Sadie clinging to his sides and back as if she were his wings. This was as close to flying as Sadie could imagine.

"Too bad you aren't showing today — you two are perfect. Great body position, good tempo, and you both look relaxed — well done. Keep up the good work, Sadie. Why don't you walk Lucky around a few more minutes to finish cooling him," her instructor suggested.

During the cooldown, Miss Kristy invited Sadie to become part of her Desire Horse Club, which meets at

Loftmar Stables on Wednesday afternoons. Sadie had seen this group, but didn't understand it. Through Desire Ministries, Miss Kristy gave children the opportunity to be around horses that may not otherwise have the chance to do so. She used horses and horsemanship to teach, mentor, train, and counsel the children. An extra hand would help Miss Kristy's club, and Sadie could start her job as a junior counselor right away.

"But let's talk terminology here for a minute," Miss Kristy began, already training her new employee. "You used the words *equine therapist*, which would mean you would be providing therapy to the horse. I don't think that's what you mean."

"No, I mean I want to help people using horses, like Goliath helped Joey."

"Good, that's what I thought, so let me explain. In our work here at the horse club we use the term equine-assisted activities. Therapeutic riding instructors also do equine-assisted activities. And in another portion of our program I will talk to you about later, we do equine- assisted therapy. It's all explained on our website, but I thought I'd explain it in person since you are here and to make sure we get started on the right track."

"Thank you, and I already know more than I did half an hour ago. I hate to be a bother, I mean, considering you hired me a minute ago. But can I ask one more question?"

"You're not a bother — remember, you are helping me," she said, reaching over to pat Lucky's neck.

"Do you think my friend, Brady, can help, too? He doesn't know much about horses, but he's eager to learn. And I know you'll like him."

"Sure. He'll be fine under your wing. This will

work great. You can help me, he can help you, and the horses can help us help the kids. What do you think?"

"I think it's a winner all the way around! Thank you, Miss Kristy!"

"Thank you, Sadie. I have to teach my next class, but I'll see you and Brady here tomorrow at 4:30, okay?"

Sadie couldn't wait to get home to tell her mom about her job. She'd send Dad an e-mail, too, since she believed he'd approve of a job. Dad was the hardest working man she knew, and he told lots of stories of growing up helping his father with his painting company. He still credited those early lessons learned with his work ethic and habits even today.

Sadie was going to begin her new career next week, learning how to help people with the help of horses. And the horses were going to help Sadie think less about her dad.

8

Sharing The News

Sadie rounded the corner from Loftmar to her house bursting into a sprint. She slowed when she saw the empty driveway, meaning no mom home to listen. Sadie's mom worked longer hours in her new job at the Office of Naval Intelligence than she had at her old accounting job. In Sadie's lifetime, Mom's job always took a backseat to Dad's career. But when opportunity knocked for Mom to work in the exciting field of intelligence, the whole family encouraged her to do something for herself — for a change.

Sadie was proud of her mom for landing this job on her own. Even though Mrs. Navarro did not make the local police happy with the way she handled a crime scene a few months back, the lead investigator detected her mom's intuition, perseverance, and planning qualities on the spot. A week after the incident, Sergeant Lucero passed Mom information on a job he thought would be a perfect fit for her. The people at the Office of Naval Intelligence in Suitland, Maryland, agreed, and Sadie's mom now served her country as a civilian intelligence officer.

But right now Sadie wanted to share her good news, and Mom wasn't home yet. And Dad was far, far away. She looked for Austin.

Knocking on his door, she started, "Austin, I have some great news…."

"I'm on the phone," he hollered. "I'll only be a few minutes." And she heard a version of boy giggling and assumed he had to be talking to Ugh Katie-bug.

"But this is *important*!"

"Okay — come in. Hold on, Katie — just for a sec?" Austin put his hand over the mouthpiece, looked at Sadie anxiously as if waiting to hear that the kitchen was on fire, and asked, "What is it?"

Feeling slightly foolish, but caught up in her moment, she blurted out, "I got a job!"

He nodded his head slightly, trying to understand, and then tilted it slightly, and said, "Okaaaay…."

"Never mind, I'll talk to you when you're not busy. I'm going to do equine-assisted activities, and I thought you'd care," she turned to leave.

"Katie, I'll call you back. Sadie, wait!" Austin called after her.

Sadie turned back and saw he regretted his disinterested reaction. He tried a second time.

"That's great! When do you start? And tell me about it." At sixteen, Austin had taken over as the man of the house in Dad's absence. And although Sadie always regarded him as her brother, sometimes she needed him to step in and listen as Dad would listen. This was one of those times, and he recognized it without being told.

"Thank you. I start tomorrow, and I'll be working with Miss Kristy's Desire Horse Club helping kids learn about horses. I'm going to be a junior counselor and one of Miss Kristy's assistants, since I know horses more than these kids do. I can't wait!"

"I saw that gleam in your eye at Maryland Therapeutic Riding, but I had no idea you would be able to get a job this fast."

"Well, I didn't tell you this before. But after we got back from Maryland Therapeutic Riding, I went online to volunteer. I was crushed when I found out I had to be fourteen. I didn't tell anyone because I felt like it was another failure."

"Don't talk like that. How can an organization's volunteer rules make you feel like a failure?"

"Oh, never mind, I can't explain the way I think sometimes. Anyhow, it's a good thing I talk a lot, because I was telling Miss Kristy, and she offered me a job with her program!"

"I think you need to tell Dad. Of course, then he'll tell me to get a job. But he knows how busy I am with track practice, and keeping you and Mom in line."

"I wanted to tell Mom, but she wasn't home. I had to tell someone. Don't you think I should tell Mom before Dad?"

"No, it would be nice for Dad to hear something first for a change. With the time difference, he may be sleeping. But at least you can try. Send Dad a note while you're still all bubbly; he'll love the good news. And then I can call Katie back, who is probably wondering what crisis developed here."

"Thanks for listening. And thank you for the advice. You're right, it will be fun to tell Dad, and I'll let him know he's first to know — well, besides you."

Sadie typed her note to Dad. It ended up being longer than she had planned. She realized she needed to give him the background on their visit to Maryland Therapeutic Riding. She tried to capture every word Miss Kristy said in relaying her story to make him feel like he was there with her. She told him she wanted to follow in her dad's footsteps and learn about working with people and the meaning of hard work at a young age so she could get better as she grew. She signed off "Your-Happily-Working-Daughter Sadie," and sat back and reread her words.

Sadie realized she felt life moving in the right direction again. Deep in thought, she looked up from the screen and found her mom standing in the doorway.

"Hi, sweetheart…is something wrong?"

"No, Mom, not at all," she smiled. Sadie hit the send button, still amazed the machine transported her thoughts to Afghanistan in seconds. "Everything is great. I have a job."

"A job?" Mom's head tilted, trying to comprehend. Sadie marveled how she had just seen that same look from her brother.

"Yes, I'm going to volunteer with a horse club right out back at Loftmar. Isn't that awesome?"

Sadie's words registered with Mom. "That's more than awesome! Tell me more as we go celebrate with a pizza. And I'm assuming you were telling Dad, right?"

"Um, yeah…I hope that's okay. I wanted to tell you first, but—"

"Don't worry. He'll be thrilled, just like I am. Don't forget to tell Grandma Collins, too. She always wants to hear the latest."

Grandma Collins. *How could Sadie have forgotten*

in her excitement to tell Grandma Collins? She would have advice for how Sadie should conduct herself in her new duties. Grandma knew something about everything, and fancied herself a horse expert, since she was the one who had chosen Lucky for Sadie. And of course Lucky turned out to be the perfect horse.

Sadie and her grandmother shared a special bond, and Grandma was never the last to learn of anything in Sadie's life. *Except for the secret Sadie kept from everyone, including Grandma Collins.*

Once in the car, Sadie dialed her grandmother in San Diego, California. Grandma picked up on the first ring.

"It's my best granddaughter!" she exclaimed.

"I'm your only granddaughter, Grandma, but thank you anyway. I have good news to share. I have you on the speakerphone so we can all visit."

"So what's the news? Blue ribbons? More horses to save? Straight A's again? The suspense is killing me!" And Sadie knew it was true.

"I am beginning my career in equine-assisted activities this week," Sadie announced, shoulders back, chin up, as if Grandma saw her through the phone. "Last weekend Austin and I witnessed how horses can help people when we went to go check on Goliath, and I decided I wanted to be a part of that world. So, I found myself a job. I'll be a volunteer, with lots to learn. But I'm happy to be starting. What do you think?"

"You never surprise me, Sadie. While most kids are playing video games and thinking about themselves, there you are trying to make the world a better place. A job! How are you going to do this and keep up with school, your riding, and all the things you still have left to do with the horses you rescued?"

"It's one day a week, Grandma. And I have time. When people want to do things, they find time. And I want to do this more than I've wanted to do anything since, well, since saving the horses. Saving horses is important, but so is helping people. And if I can do both — well, how much better can it get than that?"

Sadie watched her mom's reaction, as Mom wiped a tear. Mom gave Sadie the "sshhhh" sign, telling her not to tell her own mom how she felt.

"Tell your mom she did a heck of a job raising you," Grandma said, as if she sensed her own daughter's reaction from across the country.

"Thanks, Mom," Sadie's mom said. "But this was all Sadie. I had nothing to do with it. Well, except I reminded her she needed to follow up on the horses. Since it has made her so happy, I'm glad I was a pest."

"Where's my Austin?" Grandma asked.

"Right here, texting my girlfriend. Giving her the play-by-play of the conversation."

"Oh, you are not. You are such a joker — just like your dad."

"All right, Mom, we're at the restaurant, so we have to go now. Sadie just wanted to share her big news with one of her biggest fans."

"I appreciate it, sweetheart. Thank you for the call. And I'll send an e-mail with all the important stuff I can think of when starting a new job. You know, it wasn't long ago when I took over as president of the Over-70 Surf Club. And even though it's a volunteer job, you better believe people expected a lot out of me. But you're up for it, girl. Love you, girls, and bye, Austin!"

The Navarros celebrated over a large extra-cheese

pizza and toasted frosted root beer mugs to Sadie's new mission. Sadie wished her dad toasted with them, but didn't let worrisome thoughts preoccupy the evening. She thought instead how fortunate she was to have a support-ive family, and what she could learn in the next week to help make her a better junior counselor.

9

Teaming Up

Sadie checked her e-mail first thing in the morning, but found no response from Dad. Not so unusual. Sometimes it took days; sometimes it didn't.

But she did find an e-mail taking away some disappointment.

From: Grandma Collins
To: Sadie
Subj: TIPS ON STARTING A NEW JOB
1. Be early.
2. Listen hard.
3. Follow directions, but don't let people push you around.
4. When you're not sure what to do, smile and think. Always be nice (even if people try to push you around).
5. Ask as many questions as you need to, and when

in doubt, ask more.

Honey, I could write a book of tips, but I wanted to get this to you as soon as possible. I'm sure you will be the best worker there! Good luck, and tell me how your first day goes. I'm so proud of you!

Love you XOXO,

Grandma

Sadie sent back a short thank-you note. She loved her quirky grandma and appreciated her tips.

Waiting at the bus stop, Sadie wondered where Brady was this morning. She boarded the bus without him. Maybe his dad needed to register him on his first day in the new school? She couldn't believe he wasn't there when she wanted to share her exciting news. But hopefully she would find him later at school.

A quick glance around reminded Sadie that the people on the bus wouldn't care about her new job. So instead of being disappointed by another kid's lack of enthusiasm, she decided to bury her head in the papers she printed off about Desire Horse Club and equine activities and therapies. And she used the time to think.

Sadie always listened to her grandmother. Something Grandma said last night bugged her. What about her schoolwork? Sadie got good grades, and had to admit much of it came naturally to her. She read a lot, listened, and tried to get as much work done at school so she could spend the rest of her free time at the barn. Sadie couldn't let her current passion consume her and make her grades falter. She couldn't let her parents and her grandma down by getting less than a B or two along with straight A's.

Sadie wished she could tell her grandma that she wanted to keep as busy as she could to help her stop thinking about Dad. But she couldn't.

And, Sadie had a plan. It involved building a team and trying to link her schoolwork with her therapy work. She looked forward to sharing her thoughts with Mr. Edwards, her favorite teacher ever. Mr. Edwards made learning fun and entertaining and supported his students. Sadie understood much of her success in saving the horses in the past would not have been possible without Mr. Edwards' help.

So Sadie figured she would enlist Mr. Edwards' support in this new effort. She loved his spirit, even though he was a teacher. Other kids had him as their favorite teacher, too. Sadie heard Mr. Edwards attended functions outside the classroom for students, like seeing their plays or going to important sports events. But she also knew her teacher thought she was special. As passionate as Sadie was for horses, Mr. Edwards felt the same passion about social issues, explaining why he'd been so drawn to Sadie's first cause.

Sadie needed to convey to Mr. Edwards how important the therapy field was to her, so he would understand how she felt. She wished now she had invited him to Maryland Therapeutic Riding to see firsthand the kind of work she'd be doing. But she also realized her teacher had his own life, and she couldn't expect him to do school stuff every weekend. Besides, if she told Austin that Katie couldn't come, it wouldn't have made sense to have her teacher there as a spectator. No, she'd been right. Sadie would have to explain her interest in equine activities and therapies in her own words, and why this new job was so important to her.

Sadie sat thinking, all through class, waiting for the bell to ring dismissing her, before approaching Mr.

Edwards.

"You've been mighty quiet today, Sadie."

"Sorry. I have a lot on my mind. Do you have a minute to talk?"

"Always for you, Sadie. Let me walk to your next class with you so you're not late. It's not a secret is it?"

Sadie remembered the only secret she was keeping; she was scared to death her dad was going to get hurt. But she pushed the secret from her thoughts and focused on her request. Knowing she only had about a minute, she said, "I want to work with horses and therapy. And I need your help."

He stopped walking, and so did she. "You mean a veterinarian? That's wonderful, I can help by recommending good math and science projects, we can tailor—"

"No, not a veterinarian. I want to help people by using horses. But I don't want it to affect my schoolwork. So kind of like you were just saying, if I could work on some school papers and projects that will cover both, that would be great."

"I'm afraid to say I'm not familiar with horse therapy, but—"

"I figured you needed background, and I printed these," Sadie said, handing Mr. Edwards the stack of information. "So maybe you can take a look and we can talk more tomorrow?"

"You got it. Let me do some studying, and see what we can do."

* * *

Sadie ate lunch with her friends and listened to them discuss upcoming summer vacations. Sadie hadn't even realized she would be out of school soon, so her job shouldn't interfere too much with her schoolwork. How could she have been so stupid? Sometimes her excitement clouded her thinking, but it was too late now. Besides, summer vacation was months away, a very long time in Sadie's world these days.

"Hi, girls, how's lunch?" Mr. Edwards interrupted.

"Great — you want some?" Sadie's friend, Allie McGlade asked, holding up a cookie.

"No, but thank you. I would like to steal away your friend here for a second, if it's okay," he said, pointing to Sadie.

"Oohhh, someone's in trouble," Sadie's buddy Zoe teased.

"No she's not; you know better," Mr. Edwards responded. "We're working on a project, and I have some information that I want to share right away."

"Can we hear?" Zoe asked, big round eyes opened even wider than normal.

"Sadie?" Mr. Edwards asked.

"Sure, it's not a secret. In fact, I was looking for someone to talk to about it this morning, but didn't think anyone would care."

"Of course we care, Sadie," Allie scolded. "You listen to us. Let's hear it, Mr. Edwards."

"Let me start with the background. You see, Sadie wanted to learn about therapeutic riding. She can fill you in on the details later. So, she came to me seeing how she could maybe combine her volunteer work with a school project, which of course I thought was a great idea."

The suspense was killing Sadie. What could be so important to cause Mr. Edwards to hunt her down during lunch? And now, her friends would know, too.

"So, I looked at the information she gave me on

Desire Horse Club, and I think Sadie will do an excellent job as a junior counselor there. She knows horses, and it takes place at Loftmar Stables, which she also knows. She'll do a great job helping the kids there."

Sadie said, "Okay...."

"But this is where it gets great!" her teacher exclaimed, clenching his fist and smiling. "I figured — why not work with two programs? You can compare and contrast them, and learn so much more! Why stop at one?"

"Keep going, we want to know what you're talking about!" Zoe said.

"So, I remembered reading about a program that helped veterans, and I called them."

Fear sunk in. Sadie managed to stammer, "But, I already checked the Maryland Therapeutic Riding Horses for Heroes program, and I'm not old enough yet."

"Actually, it's a different program, and you are not old enough for this one either. But, your persuasive teacher talked to one of the founders, and she said she would take you on as a special case. Of course, I had to tell her about your past accomplishments, and that you would be doing this as a school project."

Sadie didn't want to work with veterans. She wanted to work with kids. Mr. Edwards had no idea his attempt at being helpful was feeding her terrible fears about her dad's well-being. This wasn't the distraction she had counted on.

"What's the program?" Allie asked. "And can we come, too?"

"Sadie will be working with the Caisson Platoon Equine Assisted Programs which uses Army horses and soldiers and veterans to help other veterans. Isn't that exciting?" Mr. Edwards asked, looking from face to face.

"Oh, and I'm sorry, Allie, I only made provisions for Sadie for a few visits. But maybe after her project, you can do something similar next school year, if you are interested."

Mr. Edwards zeroed in on Sadie, and said, "I thought you would be more excited, Sadie, especially since this happened so fast. I was so lucky someone answered the phone, the right person. I was astonished how it all came together so well."

Sadie swallowed to release her frozen vocal chords and managed to choke out, "Sorry — yes, that's it. It's just sudden. It's sinking in." Trying to laugh, she continued, "Yesterday I had one job, and now I have two."

"Lucky you, Sadie. And with your dad being in the Army and all," Zoe added.

"He's in the Navy," Allie corrected. "But we know what you mean. We can't wait to hear how it goes!"

Sadie saw Mr. Edwards studying her again, and she sat up straighter. She had to be strong. "When do I go?"

"Next week! I arranged for three sessions. I'll take you the first time because I really want to meet this Mary Jo Beckman in person after talking to her on the phone. She sounds like another Sadie to me. We can work out how to get you to the next two sessions later on. For now, I wanted to pass you the great news! I have to run — we'll talk more later. Goodbye, girls, and sorry to interrupt your lunch."

Sadie felt numb. Her plan backfired. She sought help, and instead would face her worst fears head on.

10

First Day on the Job

Sadie tracked down Brady at school, learning his dad had driven him in on his first day to register him in the new school. After hearing her shocking lunchtime news, Sadie was happy to explain the deal she'd arranged with Miss Kristy for Brady to help her at the horse club. Luckily, Brady had been more excited by his lunchtime news than Sadie had been with hers.

"Sadie, I think we're going to amaze ourselves today," Brady predicted on their walk up the gravel road to Loftmar Stables to their new job after school.

"You are too funny. This isn't about amazing ourselves; it's about helping out. And for me, it's getting experience in something I want to learn about," Sadie replied.

"And I think you are going to be amazing. So there."

"Okay, and I'm sure you will be amazing, too."

"I mean it. You understand horses, and how to tell

people things without making them feel stupid. I think you're going to be the best junior counselor ever."

"I'm not sure about that, but I have a good assistant," she said, nudging him.

"Do you know exactly what we'll be doing?"

"No, but I've read the information — like you have, right?" Sadie looked in Brady's direction. Brady furiously nodded his head up and down, looking comical. "And Miss Kristy will tell us what to do. She's been a teacher, so she knows how to give directions. And, there she is now. Let's go see."

"Hi, guys," Miss Kristy greeted them. Miss Kristy had the kindest voice and face. Her youthful eyes danced with inspiration on her lightly freckled round face. She wore her sandy brown hair halfway down her back in a long ponytail and wore jeans and a Desire polo shirt.

"I'm Brady, and I'm happy to be here," Brady announced.

Miss Kristy smiled and said, "I know who you are, and I am the one who is happy you are here."

Sadie watched Brady melt. He didn't seem to understand how to accept kindness.

"Where would you like us to start today?" Sadie asked.

"Marissa, could you come here for a minute, please?" An African-American girl who appeared to be around fifteen entered the barn aisle where they had been chatting. "Sadie and Brady, this is Marissa. Marissa's been with my program since she was one of my students six years ago, and now she helps me run the program."

"Wow," Brady said. "Nice to meet you, Miss Marissa."

"Oh, I'm not a Miss Marissa; you can call me Marissa. Nice to meet you, too."

Sadie detected a sadness in this girl, even though she smiled. Maybe Marissa had a bad day. Or she wasn't crazy about having to train new volunteers. Whatever it was, Sadie was going to try hard not to be a problem for Miss Kristy's helper. Sadie was here to help, and maybe even make Marissa's job easier.

"I have another volunteer here, Miss Nancy, who is with the students at the picnic table out back. Since Miss Nancy is working on a project with them, I can explain to you two more about what we do and how we do it. Marissa, can you please go tack up Snickers? We'll use him today."

And Marissa was off.

Miss Kristy started, "As I think you know, we have several missions as part of Desire Ministries. We assist in finding loving homes for horses, and we use horses and volunteers to mentor children by being a positive influence and role model to them. We work at the stable together completing barn chores and tasks teaching responsibility."

"We use the Equine Assisted Growth and Learning Association, or EAGALA, model for some of our work, to help people find hope, strength, and healing in their lives through learning and therapy with horses. And finally, we educate the public about horses, riding, and horsemanship," Miss Kristy continued.

"With our horse club, we conduct a variety of activities. Most of the children in this club have never been near horses before they come here. I emphasize this point because it will be up to you two, as volunteers, to help us keep a safe environment. Sometimes these kids get so excited that they forget they are not supposed to run or make loud noises. Although you may not like being the bad guy, I need you to enforce the rules so everyone stays safe."

"Since we have ten children, we break them up into groups when we ride. We don't ride all days, but today we will. For now, Marissa and I will take care of the riding portion. We have our routine down well after all this time. Sadie, I'll start training you to help with the riding part, too, since I know how much you know about riding."

"Hopefully I can help with that part, too, someday," Brady said, flashing a mischievous smile.

"Yes, let's hope so. But in the meantime, we have plenty of jobs. Sadie, you remember the parts of the horse, don't you? We covered it in your Certified Horsemanship Association training. It was hard, so I'm sure you haven't forgotten."

"No, I haven't forgotten. I know all fifty parts — remember, I had to take a test?"

"Good, because it's going to come in handy today. Here's what we're going to do. Marissa and I will have Snickers in the ring, and we'll bring in five of the riders. We'll let each of them ride for a few minutes, and remind them of the basics. It may not seem like a long time to you, Sadie, but for people who never ride, a few minutes is a long time. We want to slowly build up their stamina."

"Anyhow, I want you to bring Stuffy out here and put him in the cross ties. You are going to teach five students at a time about the parts of the horse."

"And I get to help?" Brady asked.

"Yes, and I already have a job for you," Miss Kristy said, handing Brady a diagram of a horse with its parts labeled, and small cards with the horse parts printed on them. "You are going to hand the students these cards, and they will place them on the right part of the horse. You can let them tape a few cards on the pony, but not too many. We don't want to make little Stuffy mad."

"Okay," Sadie said. "But can I ask a question?" Sadie remembered, Grandma Collins told her to ask lots of questions.

"Sure, please, ask all the questions you want. Both of you."

"How is this *therapy*?"

Miss Kristy smiled reassuringly. "You'll see. And remember, there are many forms of therapy — and learning — when it comes to people and horses. Be kind, but be firm, and follow your instincts. Any other questions?"

Sadie remained puzzled, but thought she'd do her best and see how it went.

Brady shook his head from side to side, signaling no, as if ready to get on with the show.

Sadie spoke for them and said, "We're ready when you are," both excited and anxious regarding her first job task.

"Great, bring Stuffy over here then. I'll send your first group out. Oh, and let the children groom the pony, too. Miss Nancy will stay with you, and I'll be right in the indoor arena. Remember to have fun."

Sadie stood Stuffy in the cross ties, and scratched his tiny head between his ears, which weren't much bigger than her pinky fingers. At 10.2 hands high, Stuffy was the smallest pony at the barn. Sadie loved him from the day he arrived, when Miss Jan bought him for her grandson, Brayden. Stuffy did a wonderful job of helping people feel comfortable around horses because of his size. He was a black and white Pony of the Americas breed, and his full name was Double Stuffed Oreo, named for the cookie. Sadie felt honored to have such a good equine companion for her first job challenge.

The ten children filed out from the picnic table area, and it was the first time Sadie had seen the group. Half of them went to the arena, and the other half came to Sadie with Miss Nancy. The first thing Sadie noticed was the number of boys in the group. Normally, around here, the girls far outnumbered the boys. The children looked to be between the ages of six and eleven, and they came in many shapes and sizes. They were Caucasian, African-American, Asian, Hispanic, and mixed, like Sadie. What an interesting group. Miss Kristy introduced Sadie and Brady to Miss Nancy, who exuded the same warmth and kindness as Miss Kristy. After the introduction, Miss Kristy left to work with the children who would ride Snickers first today. Miss Nancy told Sadie, "I'll let you do your thing and won't step in unless you ask. After all, this is for you, too."

Sadie didn't completely understand that comment, but thought perhaps she meant as part of her training to become a therapist someday.

The group of three boys and two girls stared at Sadie. Waiting.

Sadie cleared her throat and began, "Hello, boys and girls. My name is Sadie Navarro, and today—"

"How come we don't get to ride first?" interrupted the smallest girl, whose nametag read "Karla."

"I'm sorry, but I don't know the answer to that, but you'll get to ride."

"But I want to ride now."

Sadie looked at Miss Nancy, who gave her an encouraging look, but did not step in. Sadie remembered the words, kind but firm. She smiled, and said, "We can't all ride at the same time. But we're going to do something fun here, if you'll give me a chance."

Karla crossed her arms and stepped back. But at least she stopped interrupting. Sadie hated to admit that this child had flustered her.

Brady spoke up. "Who wants to start with the currycomb to groom Stuffy?"

The middle boy's hand shot up, and Brady handed him the currycomb. "Come on over here with me," and he walked with the boy in front of Stuffy, and showed him how to use the comb on his near side, opposite Sadie. Hard to believe Brady touched his first horse yesterday.

"Thank you, Brady. And I'll point to each of you when it's your turn to help groom."

"Can I pet him over here?" a low male voice asked, standing next to Sadie.

Sadie's immediate thought was, no, because she was getting distracted. But she thought about what Miss Kristy said. These kids have so little time with horses. "Sure," she said.

Sadie took a deep breath, and continued on with her lesson. She explained what they would do, and offered grooming tips to the children. Sadie hadn't done it on purpose, but once the kids recognized her horse knowledge, she earned their respect. After the grooming, they began learning the parts of the horse and laughed over the easy ones, like nostril, and appeared perplexed by the challenging ones, like stifle.

Brady handed kids the cards, and since he had the answer diagram, he offered helpful hints when needed. While Karla hovered near the top of Stuffy's back, with her card that read "barrel," Brady looked down, and down again, until Karla figured out that he was trying to help. As soon as she placed the card in the right place on the pony's belly, Brady said, "Bingo!" and they all laughed.

After the first group finished riding, Sadie started the lesson again. She'd learned a thing or two in that short session. Sadie felt less anxious this time, and Brady enjoyed being on stage and helping teach kids how to groom. Brady even showed a boy, Tyler, how to pick a hoof.

"Stuffy's hoof is much smaller than Lucky's," the experienced-hoof-picker Brady shared with Tyler. Brady coached his student much like Sadie had coached him the day before.

The children focused on learning the parts of the horse, and asked lots of good questions, such as, "Why do they call it that?"

When Sadie didn't know one of the answers, she said, "I don't know, but I'll find out and tell you next week."

A big girl with a slight lisp said excitedly, "You mean you are coming back to teach us more and help us again?"

Sadie nodded, looked at Brady, and said, "Wouldn't miss it for the world." She also understood, less than one hour into her first job, why Miss Nancy said this was for her, too.

11

Horses and Veterans

The day arrived sooner than Sadie wanted for her arranged internship with the Caisson Platoon Equine Assisted Programs. At the end of the school day, Mr. Edwards headed with Sadie for Fort Myer in Arlington, Virginia, for her first day with the program.

Mr. Edwards worked with Sadie so much during her horse rescue operation that her mom considered him not just Sadie's teacher, but a family friend. Sadie never abused this privilege. Even though Sadie wasn't happy that her teacher got her into this fearful predicament, she still looked forward to the time with him. Soon, the school year would be over, and she didn't think she'd ever have a teacher she could learn so much from again.

They arrived at the Caisson Platoon horse stables, and Mrs. Mary Jo Beckman met them at the entrance. Her warmth made Sadie's fears somewhat subside right away. Petite, with glasses and shoulder-length brown hair, Mrs.

Beckman's concerned face showed she'd helped many a veteran. If she sensed Sadie's nervousness, she did not let on. Sadie loved the way the program's founder treated her like an adult. And she appreciated the soft-spoken manner in which this leader relayed as much information as humanly possible in a short period of time.

The three toured the stable, and Sadie had never seen a cleaner barn. Over ten men in their late teens and early twenties swept up the few out-of-place errant pieces of hay and dusted gleaming stained wood stall doors. The workers polished black bars above the stall doors over which the Caisson Platoon horses hung their heads out for a visit.

Mrs. Beckman explained, "Soldiers of the U.S. 3rd Infantry Division's 'Old Guard' man the unit, and take care of the horses and this stable. Some have previous horse experience, and some do not." It was clear to Sadie the soldiers all emanated pride in their duty.

Sadie examined the soldiers' sharp uniforms — long-sleeved black shirts with white embroidered unit information, names, and ranks. They wore white cowboy hats, blue jeans, and stylish black cowboy boots. Sadie noticed most of their clothing matched the two colors of the unit horses — black and white. One of the soldiers stopped to talk to Mrs. Beckman about the adaptive carriage unit used as part of the therapy program. He noticed Sadie checking out his uniform.

"Do you like these?" the soldier smiled and asked, pointing to his shirt.

"Yes, I do," Sadie answered, admiring the crisp creases on the sleeves and wondering how he kept his hat so white while working in a barn.

"We do, too. They are new. We started attending

Clinton Anderson clinics to help our horse training. Someone suggested it might make more sense for our uniform to be more practical for what we do. Our bosses convinced their bosses, and now we're dressed better to work with horses than when we wore BDUs and combat boots." In reaction to Sadie's face crinkling, he added, "That's battle dress uniforms."

"I remember now. My dad wears them. He's in the Navy, but he's in Afghanistan."

The soldier nodded, "I understand. You all take care now, and enjoy your visit." He tipped his hat and strode off to his chores.

"Mrs. Beckman," Sadie asked, "are there any girl soldiers in the Caisson Platoon?"

Mrs. Beckman thought for a minute. "Not now, Sadie, but there was one female soldier here, Sergeant Mullen, when we started the program. She was my point of contact for organizing the lessons. And maybe there will be more someday."

Mrs. Beckman described the horses — all draft horses or half-draft horses. They required precise training to perform their mission serving in funeral processions honoring fallen servicemen and servicewomen. One of the reasons the Caisson Platoon horses made great therapy horses was due to their job training. The soldiers taught them to stand still. When on funeral duty, the horses often left the barn at eight o'clock in the morning and did not return until 3:30 in the afternoon. The horses' patience, training, and sizes suited them well to therapy work.

Mr. Edwards stared at the surroundings, wide-eyed and asked, "How about the history of your therapy program here?"

"The Caisson Platoon Equine Assisted Programs

began as an all-volunteer effort to offer equine-assisted therapy to amputee patients at Walter Reed National Military Medical Center. All at no cost to the individuals. Since 2006, wounded warriors and veterans have benefitted from the Caisson Platoon horses."

Mrs. Beckman continued, "As a master therapeutic riding instructor, I knew the physical benefits of equine therapy. I also understood the mental and emotional benefits for participants. I was fortunate to partner with Larry Pence, a retired Army command sergeant major. The two of us cofounded the program to engage wounded military members through equine-assisted activities in the Washington, D.C., area. As veterans, Larry and I recognized the value of military members serving as horse leaders and side-walkers during sessions, which serves as a key strength of the program."

"So, your volunteers need to be soldiers?" Sadie asked. She tried to chase away the little red devil on her shoulder. He whispered, *You may be able to duck out now and not face your fears of working with the wounded!"*

"No, not all volunteers are soldiers."

The devil disappeared in a poof.

The program cofounder continued, "We like to use soldiers as side-walkers and horse leaders here because we know our clients identify with them. We've found when soldiers help other soldiers, or military members of any service, it helps them, too. Our volunteers help in many ways — in preparing for sessions, administrative work, and even just talking to the veterans. There is plenty of work to go around — don't you worry."

Sadie smiled, surprising herself.

Mr. Edwards asked, "Can you tell us how your work expanded to programs across the country? I find it fascinating, and something I try to teach my kids. When you do something powerful enough at the grassroots level, you can lead great change across the nation." Sadie smiled again, listening to Mr. Edwards provide Mrs. Beckman a short class on middle school social studies in case she'd forgotten.

"When the Secretary of Veterans Affairs visited the program in 2006, he recognized its potential for veterans everywhere. So, Larry and I met with the Veterans Affairs staff, and with officials from the Professional Association of Therapeutic Horsemanship (PATH) International."

"And you are a member of PATH International, too, right?" Sadie asked. "In fact, I remember reading in your biography that you won a lifetime achievement award from them last year."

"Well, I see you've done your homework." A flush crept across the coy woman's cheeks. "Yes, I've been a member of PATH for years. It's one of the reasons I knew how valuable this therapy could be for many populations. Now, back to our program here, our work together resulted in the Equine Services for Heroes program. That program now includes over 100 PATH International centers nationwide working with local veterans' medical centers. Veterans from World War II, the Korean War, Vietnam, Desert Storm, Iraq, and Afghanistan take part, using the "Soldiers helping Soldiers" concept.

"Over 100 centers? Believe it or not, I got to visit one, at Maryland Therapeutic Riding. It's how I ended up here, in a roundabout way," Sadie said, looking toward Mr. Edwards, who seemed to be enjoying his student's learning experience.

"Many of the programs vary in what they offer, and I'd encourage you to check them out in your continuing research. Around the country, many of the horse leaders and side-walkers serve in local National Guard and Reserve units. This situation provides veteran clients continued contact with fellow service members who speak their language and understand their experiences. The service member volunteers cite the value of the program to them in taking care of their own, like the soldiers in the Old Guard. Today, thousands of military, veterans, and families have participated in equine programs due to this expansion."

"Mrs. Beckman, I hate to keep asking questions, and I know you are very busy...."

"Sadie, ask away. I'm happy someone your age is interested in the program and willing to help. My daughters started at your age, and they learned a lot. I made the time to meet with you today to introduce you to the program and give you the background. We won't have any participants coming today, so I'm yours."

She continued, "As you may know, we are in the final stages of moving our operation to Fort Belvoir. So your next visits will be there. My friend Captain Vinson will be putting you to work in the program. So please, ask me whatever you'd like to know since I may not see you again in your internship. I thought it would be good for us to meet here, where it all started, and where you could see the actual Caisson Platoon, and the important mission that these horses have."

"Thank you, and I appreciate it. I'll try to be quick," Sadie said, looking at Mr. Edwards, who told her not to take too much of the generous cofounder's time. "Here's one of my prepared questions." Sadie pulled her pen and notebook out and read, "Could you please share with me the top three points you would like me to get across in my paper and to the public about your program?"

"Excellent question. Let me see if I can limit it to three. First, we want people to understand that horses help people. Horses can be so calming. I've seen people walk in, and as soon as they are around the horses they gain a heightened awareness. Horses can cause a change in a person's body posture from stiff to relaxed in an instant. Am I talking too fast?" she asked, as Sadie scribbled.

"No, ma'am. I'm keeping up. Please continue."

"So there is an emotional side of equine therapy. But there are also huge physical benefits. We start with ground work. But when a person does ride, the rider's body moves as if walking normally. Riding improves balance, movement, and core strength. The movement allows the body to feel as if it is taking steps. Riders have told us by sitting on a horse, they feel as if they have taken thousands of good steps. Horses move side to side and up and down, and the constant balancing motion develops core stability. The actions teach people how to use their bodies again. We do tests, and people can tell a difference, even after the first ride."

"Can you give me a particular example I can cite in my paper?" Sadie asked.

Mrs. Beckman ran her hand across her chin and answered, "I can think of many. But one of the most powerful statements came from a client who said he could live without pain for a short time while riding. In other words, the only time he wasn't in pain, was while on the horse. Can you imagine?" Sadie could read the pain in Mrs. Beckman's face as she relayed the story.

"I've spoken about the emotional and physical benefits, and the third would be the cognitive. We teach people about horses, and grooming, and tack. These are new to many people. We also teach riding skills, and our students do exercises requiring them to think about what they are doing and how to work with the horse. For many of our participants with traumatic brain injury or dealing with post-traumatic stress disorder symptoms, these basic thinking skills are a necessary beginning. Even something as basic as learning how to control a horse's feet can pose quite a challenge."

Sadie saddened, considering a grown man or woman struggling to concentrate to make a horse move in the right direction.

"And if you let me relay a fourth point, I need to mention the social benefits of the program for the individuals. Besides what I've said about the soldiers being with their own, including the soldier horses, our program gets many of these people out who may not otherwise get out. So many of the patients at the medical centers become so isolated. Many of them say being here is their favorite part of the week, and they look forward to it. And that's what we would hope for."

"Time for my last question, I promise. Is there anything else you would like to share with me today?" Sadie asked.

"We really need more good research to prove the capabilities of equine therapy programs. We know what good they do, and our students understand, but often, the medical documentation is difficult. Last year, Larry and I decided to use Caisson Platoon Equine Assisted Programs funds to help initiate a research project to promote research to quantify and qualify how equine-assisted activities and therapies benefit the military population and veterans. We focused on those suffering from traumatic brain injuries and post-traumatic stress disorder, but we need much more. We continue to work with equine research organizations, colleges, universities, and institutions to validate equine programs, but it's an area where more work needs to be done."

"Wow," Sadie said. "Well, I sure hope I can help somehow. I'll do my best."

"Thank you, Sadie, and I believe you will. Now, before you go, let me show you a few more things to help prepare you for next week's visit." They walked to a small tack room, and Mrs. Beckman pulled out several pieces of leather tack adapted for use by those with balance issues. "The tack is handmade right here by the Army, and it's excellent quality. This is what we call a rein handle, and it allows a rider to control both reins with the use of one hand, or prosthetic."

Sadie began to get squeamish, and tried not to show it.

"Are you ready to go meet some Caisson Platoon horses?" Mrs. Beckman asked.

"Yes!" Sadie answered, in half a second.

They strolled the pristine stable aisles, and Mrs. Beckman told stories now and then about particular horses. Each horse was more picture-perfect than the next. Their coats glistened like dress uniforms, and each one appeared as fit as a warrior. Sadie loved reading their names...Klinger, King, Silver...so majestic. Mrs. Beckman completed the tour by showing them the main tack room, in which every spotless bridle, harness, and saddle hung in its proper place. Sadie thought her dad would love the order in this place.

As they left, Mr. Edwards said, "Thank you so much for your valuable time, Mrs. Beckman. You've added so much to Sadie's research, and I'm excited for the future of her project. She's a go-getter, and she wasn't kidding when she said she would do what she could do. You'll be glad she's on your side!" he finished, with his normal enthusiasm.

"Thank you, ma'am. I learned a lot. It's been an honor to meet you," Sadie said, looking into the admirable woman's eyes and feeling ashamed she didn't embody the same bravery this woman exhibited. She knew she needed to find it before next week.

"It's been my pleasure, and I wish you the best in the rest of your project. I hope you can join us in the program in a few years. Captain Vinson will take good care of you, but if you have any questions, please contact me. Same for you, Mr. Edwards, and thank you for arranging this visit. We need more teachers like you." And she waved goodbye as they departed the stables.

Sadie and Mr. Edwards headed for his car, and Sadie's thoughts reeled from the past hour. She wanted to help, but worried. How would she deal with injured veterans, and things she didn't understand? She heard the unmistakable clip-clop of horses' hooves on pavement, and scanned the gray day looking for the source. Horses calmed people. Mrs. Beckman said so. Sadie knew it. And she needed calming.

She followed the directional sound of the methodical clip-clopping hooves. Sadie watched a team of spit-shined Caisson Platoon horses pull an immaculate well-kept antique caisson wagon carrying a coffin. This wasn't how she imagined learning about equine therapy, and she questioned whether she faced more than she could handle.

Sadie followed Mr. Edwards, who rushed to the car so he could rehash their meeting. "Wow! That was even better than I imagined. I knew from talking to Mrs. Beckman on the phone that she would be helpful. What a dedicated veteran giving back to fellow veterans. And you've met her, and learned from her. I'm so excited for you. I'm sorry you won't be coming back here, but I have a great feel for the rest of the internship. Don't you?"

Sadie still couldn't believe she hid her cards so well, but she guessed she did. She tried to think of something positive to say so as not to disappoint Mr. Edwards, who thought he was doing everything to help her. She continued staring at the caisson carrying the coffin off into the distance toward Arlington Cemetery for its burial.

"Yes, Mr. Edwards, I learned a lot." Sadie took a deep breath to compose herself and looked away from the coffin. "And it's okay we are not coming back here for the rest of the project. I saw more than I thought I would see." Although she felt gratitude for what her teacher had done, she still couldn't bring herself to thank him for intensifying her hidden fears.

12

The First Show

A swarm of bees buzzed in Sadie's stomach sending tingling sensations to all her extremities. Her nerves surprised her. Sadie competed once before in Loftmar's in-house show, but this was a very different scene. At Loftmar, she knew everyone, rode in her own familiar arena, and shared friendly camaraderie with her fellow competitors. The Maryland Horse Show series at the Prince George's Equestrian Center made the Loftmar show look like Little League baseball compared to the World Series.

The equestrian center spread across 200 acres including an indoor riding arena, two outdoor riding rings, a brand-new covered outdoor arena, and two designated schooling areas. The center occupied the grounds of the former Marlboro Race Track where thoroughbreds raced years ago. The historic track barns included 400 concrete stalls for the horses, and renovated bathrooms and showers that famous jockeys had used. The facility included an actual dirt racetrack where horse-driving events occurred, a huge water tower with a lovely horse painting on it, and a giant electronic billboard announcing the ongoing show for passersby to see. The enormity of it all rattled Sadie, and she regretted not having come here before today to get an idea of what she was in for.

Still early, horses nickered in their stalls, some stamped their hooves and banged on doors, and others stood patiently. Large banners representing different barns adorned sections of the stables, and hundreds of parents, siblings, friends, and fans decorated the scene with fold-up chairs, coolers, and snacks. For some reason, Sadie envisioned this show as much smaller. But it was too late to turn back now.

"Sadie!" Coach Amanda hollered, bringing her out of her trance while Sadie was examining the huge outdoor riding rings. "We need you over here. Time's getting tight, and we still have lots to do."

Sadie shuffled over, eyes still on the oversized riding rings in the distance.

"Are you okay?" Amanda asked.

"Um, yeah, sure."

"Because you don't look it. What's wrong?"

"Nothing really. I guess I just didn't realize how big this show was. I've never done anything like this."

"Well, that's why I'm here — remember — Coach Amanda. I wouldn't put you in any situation you couldn't handle. You're ready for this. Come on over with the rest of the group. This may be your first big show, but we're all in this together."

Amanda turned away and gestured for her student to follow. Sadie couldn't figure out why she was so nervous, but somehow she felt that the past few minutes she'd spent alone at this place had been hours.

"There you are!" Mom called, smiling and gently wiping Lucky's face with a small damp rag. Whenever Lucky stood in a stall, his head hung out, savoring any bit of attention, even having his face wiped.

"All right, everybody, listen up," Amanda commanded, speaking to the assembled group. This spring and summer, four riders from Loftmar were competing in the Maryland Horse Show series. Jessica would be riding Loftmar's PayDay, or Snickers as they called him; Erin on Loftmar's Better Than Ever, or Everett; Jimmy on his own horse, Billy Walkabout; and Sadie on Color Me Lucky. All the horses had show names and go-by names, and each horse had its own personality, just like each rider.

"We'll be competing in three different divisions today, and only two of you will be competing against each other. So, let's try to help each other out when we can. For instance, this is Sadie's first show, guys, and I'm sure you remember how that was."

Ohhh — why did she have to tell everyone? Well, she guessed they knew she hadn't been here before. Captain Obvious.

"I'll help her," Jimmy volunteered.

"We'll help, too," Jessica said, pointing to Erin as part of the *we*. "It will be less boring that way."

Boring! With Sadie's heart in her throat and those bees still buzzing in her torso, Sadie couldn't understand how anyone could find this boring.

"Great — thanks then, and listen for the line-up," Amanda continued, tapping her clipboard. "Jessica, you'll be going first this morning in your flat classes, classes 101 through 103. So follow me down to the schooling ring as soon as we're finished here. After this morning's division, you'll have a big break before this afternoon's jumping classes."

"Like I said — boring," Jessica said, snickering and rolling her eyes.

"Excuse me, I'm trying to listen," Sadie's mom said.

Sadie wished her mom hadn't just "shhh'ed" the senior rider, and she hoped Jessica wouldn't hold it against her. Exchanging a blushing embarrassed glance with Jessica, Sadie realized it was okay.

"Since you'll be so bored, Jessica, make sure to check all the horses' water and hay in your spare time," no-nonsense Amanda continued. "Erin and Jimmy, you're next, in classes 104 through 106, and then you two have a break. Basically, you'll be following right after Jessica, so that will be easy. We'll have a couple of minutes to school, or practice, ahead of time, but I want you to school a little on your own, too. You know what to do."

"Good," Erin said. She talked less than most barn kids. And her mom stood next to her nodding, knowingly.

"Sadie, you are in the last classes before lunch, so you'll have plenty of time to observe."

"And get nervous," Sadie quipped.

"I'll have none of that out of you. You're an excellent rider, you have a great horse, and this isn't any different than being at home, except for more people. Now I've gotta go and get ready for the first class. Mrs. Navarro, you got her?" Amanda quizzed, looking in Sadie's mom's direction.

"Yes, Amanda, I have her. She'll be fine. For such a confident kid, I don't know why she gets like this."

"Um...I'm right here, ya know."

"Okay, and hey, come watch the classes, and you'll

77

see how easy it is," Amanda said while walking toward the area where riders continued to school their horses, getting them accustomed to the surroundings.

If only Amanda knew that Sadie felt like losing her breakfast right now, and the first class hadn't even begun.

13

Butterflies Rising

Mom put her arm around Sadie. "Let's go make one more check on Lucky. Then we can wander down and watch Jessica to give you an idea of how it's done. C'mon, Sadie, you'll be fine."

"I *won't* be fine. Somehow this isn't what I expected. Do you see all the people here? They'll all be looking at *me*!"

Walking the row of stalls, passing horses' heads hanging out for attention, Sadie's mom slowed. She patted a needy pony, and replied, "I'm sorry to break it to you, sweetheart." She cracked a small smile. "They're not all here to see you."

Sadie stopped in her tracks. Yes, perhaps she was being irrational. But she was almost thirteen, and that came with the territory. "Maybe you're right," she managed to force out.

The four Loftmar horses lived next to each other while stabled at the show, which they liked. Horses, herd creatures by nature, find comfort in groups, especially in groups of horses they know. Lucky was housed right next to Billy, like at Loftmar, and Sadie enjoyed this arrangement, too. This meant she would be right next to Jimmy. And after all, he offered to help her today. As they approached Lucky to check on him, Sadie heard rustling inside his stall. Peering in, she found a sight to behold.

"At your service, ma'am!" piped up an excited Brady, as he stood at attention. Clad in knickers, a button-down shirt, and a plaid fisherman's cap, Brady held a soft brush at his side while wearing a huge grin.

"What are *you* doing here?" Sadie asked, curious, but happy.

"Isn't it obvious? I came to be your groom."

Explains the get-up, Sadie considered. He must have seen it in a movie. Sadie doubted she'd see any other grooms in similar attire, but she loved the fact that he cared so much to look the part.

"Well, of course it's obvious now. And you are hard at work. But Brady, you really shouldn't have gone in there without me around."

"Really? Wow, sorry. It's just that since Lucky knew me, I wanted to surprise you by having him clean. And his tack box was here, and I knew what to do. Sorry, Sadie, I was trying to help," Brady said, shoulders drooping.

"Come on out and let's talk. I'm not mad. I appreciate what you were trying to do. You didn't understand — that's my fault. I need to teach you more. Another great reason you are here!"

Brady exited the stall, deflated, and Sadie felt sorry for him. She wondered if Amanda felt bad when she had to tell students things they didn't want to hear. She knew she had to make it right — poor, sensitive Brady.

"How did you get here?" Sadie asked, changing the subject.

"My dad dropped me off. Do you think I can get a ride home with you?"

"Your dad dropped you off and left?!" Sadie's mom asked in disbelief.

"Yes, after I begged and begged him, he said if it would shut me up he would take me here. And so I'm here. I wasn't sure where you were. But I found Lucky easily. I thought I'd start brushing him so Sadie could do more important things."

"Brady, that is so sweet of you. Of course you can ride home with us. I'll need to talk to your dad about leaving you here, though. I know you are new to the area, but that's really just not safe."

"Please don't get me in trouble, Mrs. Navarro," Brady begged. "Besides, my dad won't be there by the time we get home."

"Um, folks, we can talk about this later…we're here for a horse show," Sadie reminded.

"That's why I'm here!" Brady chimed in, visibly happy to discuss the show instead of his dad.

Sadie's mom shook her head, still looking disturbed by Brady's dad's actions, but probably willing to let it go for the time being to make Sadie happy.

"Brady, since you did such a good job cleaning up Lucky, let's go see the first classes now. We can come back later and do the finishing touches together — deal?"

"Deal," he answered.

"Why don't you kids go along, and I'll stay here with Lucky a bit longer."

"Thanks, Mom. I'm sure Lucky appreciates the company." Sadie squeezed her mom's hand. She was grateful her mom did not drop her off here in this strange place with hundreds of people.

Sadie and Brady trod the path between the stables and the outdoor rings, 100 yards away, listening to the announcements over the public address system. "Ring one, all walk, please; ring one, all walk. Ring two, rising trot; ring two, rising trot. Class number 101, calling all entries for class number 101 in ring one." Sadie wondered how people kept the directions straight. The noise sounded distracting and confusing.

The sun warmed them, and a slight breeze circulated the smells of horse barns, wet pavement from horse baths, and the center's greasy breakfast fare. Horses clip-clopped on the their way to and from the rings, trailer doors opened and shut, and coaches hollered in the distance providing last-minute advice to their students. The atmosphere was carnival-like without the rides.

"Have you been to a horse show, Brady?"

"Are you kidding me? Of course not. I have to say, this is eventful! But it must be old hat for you."

"To tell you the truth, this show is my first. Well, except the small show at Loftmar for students. But I've never been to a big show like this."

"No! Aren't you scared?"

"Wanna know a secret?"

"Of course I do! I love secrets!"

"I'm not surprised. Well, here's my secret. Yes, I was very scared. Until you came. Somehow, you made all the scariness go away, and now I'm going to be just fine."

"I did that?" he asked, eyes widening.

"Yes, you did, Brady Brogan."

"Wow."

"Wow is right, and thanks. Hey, there's the Loftmar people. Let's go see what they're doing."

The two fell into place beside Amanda and Erin, watching along the fence line. Amanda kept her eyes peeled on the ring and said, "Hi, Sadie — Jessica is in this class. It's a few levels up from yours, so don't freak. But pay attention. It's all about learning."

"Thanks, Coach. Coach Amanda, this is my friend, Brady. And Erin, this is Brady."

Amanda gave a quick sideways glance to acknowledge the introduction, and then turned back. "Aren't you adorable?" she said, eyeing Brady's outfit.

Brady blushed a shade of red matching one of the stripes in his plaid cap. "Thank you, ma'am. And I'm not just Sadie's friend, I'm her groom."

"That's so sweet. Nice to meet you, Brady, and hope to see you around more."

Erin nodded, as if everyone else came with his or her own groom. Oh, Sadie pondered, it must be so difficult to be fifteen and too cool to talk anymore.

Brady whispered in Sadie's ear, "I think your coach likes me." Sadie smiled in agreement.

Sadie observed the action in the ring. She counted fifteen horses and riders keeping perfect spacing of at least one horse length apart in the large ring. She wondered how anyone could judge this class because all the riders were so good. They moved at the rising trot, effortlessly rising and falling to the horses' strides, hands in the right place, heels down, and eyes up, as they were supposed to be. Sadie found Jessica and zeroed in on her.

As Jessica passed, she caught Sadie's eye and mouthed the word "eeeaaassssy" to her. Fortunately

Coach Amanda hadn't seen, because although Sadie felt better, talking to the audience while being judged was not good show etiquette. Brady chuckled, and Sadie poked him in the ribs. He looked at her like "what?" Sadie gave him the "shhh" sign. She'd explain later.

"Ring one, all canter; ring one, all canter, please," came the woman's radio announcer style voice over the loudspeaker, echoing across the grounds.

Things in the ring weren't looking as easy now. Some transitioned to the canter easier than others, and the faster speed of the gait highlighted bigger differences in the horses and riders. Some pairs traveled slowly at the three-beat gait between a trot and a gallop, and others moved along at a more frenzied pace. Horses in groups tend to want to chase each other, and this ring included chasers. In this particular class, the point was to try to make the ride look pleasurable. Some succeeded; some didn't.

Sadie felt for those who looked terrified and wondered why they were out there. She heard the voices from sidelines ranging from support to downright yelling. She spotted one girl on a big gray mare coming toward her, with her teeth clenched, eyes wide, and body stiff as a board. Their eyes met, and Sadie mouthed the word "ee-aassyy" to her, and gave her the thumbs-up sign, which came to her by habit.

"Ring one, all walk; ring one, all walk, and change directions, please," from the omniscient announcer.

As the girl on the gray mare passed at the walk, she looked down, verging on tears, and said "Thank you," to Sadie, who nodded, hoping she had done for this girl what Brady had done for her.

Brady looked up at Sadie and patted her on the

back. "I think this is going to be your day, Sadie."

"It already has been, Brady. It already has been."

14

Blast from the Past

"Where's Jimmy?" Sadie asked Erin, trying not to sound too anxious.

"Over there," she nodded to the opposite side of the ring, toward the small metal bleachers. Nothing excited her.

Sadie headed over to Jimmy, spotting his straight brown hair. After all, Jimmy was going to help her get ready. Brady followed in tow. As she got closer, she noticed a strange girl tossing her long dark hair and letting out a phony feminine laugh. Sadie swore she was posing.

"Hey, what's up? You have this figured out yet?" Jimmy asked Sadie, friendly as always.

Before Sadie responded, the poser interrupted, "Who's the elf?" Pointing her nose in Brady's direction.

Sadie said the first thing that popped into her mind. "What?" *Brilliant.*

The rude girl laughed her evil little fake laugh

again and said, "You heard me, I asked who's the elf?"
Something about this girl was familiar.

"Now Rachel, that's not nice. It's obvious to me
this is Sadie's groom. Now just because you don't have
one is no reason to get nasty," Jimmy said jokingly...or
flirty?

RACHEL! That's who this person was. Sadie remem-
bered her from the time she shopped for a home for Lucky last
summer. Rachel wasn't nice then, either. What was she doing
here? With her.... friend? Her barn mate? And she looked dif-
ferent.

"Hi, I'm Brady Brogan. And like he said, I'm Sadie's groom." He held out his small hand for a handshake,
which Rachel ignored. Brady didn't appear bothered by
her attempted insults. He looked at her as if he felt sorry
because she didn't know what a groom looked like or understand people are supposed to shake hands.

"Well, Jimmy, maybe you can be my groom?"
Again, with the head toss and this time, a cackle. *How did*
she fit so much tossy hair in a helmet anyhow?

"I need to get to my grooming. Coach Amanda
will have my you-know-what if I'm not ready on time.
There's only two more classes in this division. Later, Rachel. Sadie, you want to stay here and watch some more,
or come with me back to the barn?"

In a nanosecond Sadie answered, "I'll come with
you."

"Okay, well then buh-bye, Loftmar buddies. Don't
want to get in trouble with your little coach now, do you?"
the rude girl continued, waving her hand backwards as if
dismissing the group.

Heading back to the stalls, as soon as they were
out of earshot, Sadie asked, "Do you know her?"

"We're in the same grade, so I've seen her at school. She seems very independent."

Independent? Mean-spirited came more to mind.

"Do you really think she was jealous because she didn't have her own groom?" Brady asked.

Jimmy caught Sadie's eye and winked at her without letting Brady see. "Of course she was — hey, even I'm jealous. But maybe you'll help me, too, ya think?" he teased.

"Of course I'll help, even though we haven't been properly introduced."

"I'm sorry, Brady, I thought you two met at the barn. Where're my manners? Jimmy, meet my friend, neighbor, and now, groom, Brady. This is his first show, too."

"Stick with me, kid; I'll show you the ropes. I've been to enough of these shows to know what to do next, and next, and next," Jimmy said.

"As long as Sadie says it's okay. She is my priority."

Sadie loved this kid. Sometimes he sounded so adult. "Of course it's okay, we all help each other anyway."

The group stood in front of Billy's stall, and Jimmy looked to be inventorying his tack. Sadie said, "I'll give Billy a quick touch-up."

"Remember how ticklish Billy is? For a big horse, he's goofy about certain things. But I wouldn't give him up for anything," Jimmy said, admiring his handsome bay quarter horse.

Sadie slid into the stall and used a soft brush to get the invisible dusting of dirt off Billy's silky dark brown coat. She laughed as the horse put his ears back and looked at her as if saying, "Stop tickling me." She was glad Jimmy reminded her, or else she would have wondered why Billy reacted that way. Most horses liked being groomed.

Brady helped Jimmy tack up, and Sadie helped Jimmy into his classy tailored navy blue show jacket. Jimmy seemed bigger in his fancy jacket and tall black show boots, and Sadie had to admit, he looked great. She'd never seen him dressed in this kind of outfit. He tied his tie, like she'd seen her dad do so many times, which seemed so odd. Jimmy belonged in jeans and T-shirts, not jackets and ties. And why did she care so much about his apparel?

Continuing an earlier conversation, Sadie said, "I met that girl last summer. But she looked kind of different."

"You mean Rachel?"

"Yes, her."

"That's a pretty good memory to remember someone you met a year ago."

"I saw her for a couple of minutes at a barn we visited to check on boarding Lucky. She ignored me, flirted with Austin, and tried to make us believe she owned the farm. Difficult to easily forget."

"Are you sure it was her?"

"She looks different, maybe it's the clothes, or the hair, I don't know."

"Ha! It may be the hair. She told me she dyed her hair to match her horse's coat. Isn't that crazy?"

Crazy and stupid, Sadie wanted to say. Everyone wore helmets these days, so who would see her matching hair when she rode anyhow?

"Oh well, enough about her. Brady, toss me my helmet, will you? Thanks," Jimmy said, catching his helmet.

Brady appeared thrilled with his new assignment.

Jimmy snapped the clasp on his helmet and asked, "So, how do I look?"

Sadie looked him up and down, and wanted to answer, "Great!" But instead, "different," came out.

"That's good, because I don't want to wear clothes like this every day. Let's head to the action. I still need to school Billy and work out his kinks. C'mon, Erin, let's go."

Sadie had forgotten Erin, oops. It must have shown in her face because Jimmy offered, "Erin and her mom have this routine down, too. They are pros, and don't need help, like me," and he flashed his perfect white teeth which stood out against his tan face.

The whole group headed for the outdoor schooling rings. Amanda remained in the same spot at the fence, and Jessica participated in one of her final classes. Amanda held Jessica's ribbons for her while she continued showing, and Jessica had done well. And she'd made it look easy. Sadie needed to figure out the easy part.

As soon as Jessica's class finished, Amanda took Jimmy and Erin over to the schooling ring, where participants practiced before their official classes. Jimmy joked around, and Erin looked as if nothing fazed her. Sadie guessed experience helped, but personalities mattered, too. She looked at Brady, remembered how much her funny little friend calmed her, took a deep breath, and relaxed. It was going to be fine.

Sadie's mom joined them watching the practice rides and said, "The horses all are behaving well today, aren't they?"

"They sure are," Amanda answered. "Some horses enjoy showing off; it's as if they get that it's important.

We're having a good day. And we're going to keep it that way." Amanda looked over her glasses in Sadie's direction, aiming the comment at her.

"Okay, let's go, guys, they're calling for your classes' entries," Amanda called.

Jimmy and Erin entered the arena, along with twelve other horses and excellent riders. Sadie couldn't help but look for Rachel, but didn't find her. Billy looked spectacular, with his black mane, tail, and legs glistening in the sun and his dark brown body showing every muscle. Billy may not like being groomed, but he liked the show ring.

Sadie recognized Jimmy's dad, who arrived the minute Jimmy's class began. He waved at the Loftmar group, and remained a ways off, talking on his cell phone. Sadie tried to remember a time she saw him without it. She couldn't.

"How come there's not more boys here?" Brady asked, looking confused.

"It's actually 'How come there aren't more boys here,' but good question. When I lived in California, more guys rode, but most of them were cowboys, or cowboy wannabes. There are a few guys here. Maybe they are just the brave ones."

"I want to ride. I think I can do what they are doing in there."

"I'm sure you can, and we'll get you lots of practice before your first show. How does that sound?"

"Awesome! I'm going to be in a show...but wait, who will be your groom? No, I need to be your groom. Next year, okay?" His eyes lit up.

"Another deal."

The riders continued around the ring, trotting

now, and the steering was worse than the last class. Riders rode next to each other, and one cut through the center close to running over the judge. Oh, that couldn't be good. At least the rider wasn't Jimmy or Erin. The command for the group to canter came over the loudspeaker. Sadie wondered if she would find a rider to help in this class.

The group cantered in one direction for too long, Sadie thought. She scanned faces looking for who needed encouragement. Jimmy came by grinning at the Loftmar group, not a care in the world. Erin looked so deep in concentration it scared Sadie. Erin's riding position looked perfect. Sadie tried to imagine herself looking the same; it was called "visualizing."

"All walk; ring one, all walk, please, and reverse directions," commanded the loudspeaker. "Ring two, rider number 276, you may begin your course." The nonstop chatter still unsettled Sadie. "Ring one, all canter; ring one, canter." The announcer directed actions in three different rings at a time. Sadie wondered how the riders kept track of who was supposed to do what.

Boy, how quick, Sadie thought. *The riders didn't even have time to catch their breath from cantering.*

Sadie watched the horses and riders in ring one picking up speed. Some riders cantered on the rail, and a few began to cut corners to keep from running up on other riders. The next thing Sadie heard was a loud crack, followed by a flash of white careening around the ring, riderless. A blood curdling scream followed, and the judge in the ring and several coaches on the sidelines hollered, "All halt! Halt!"

The spectators murmured things like "Did you see what happened?" and "Where is she?"

One only had to listen in the direction of the loud

wails and crying to see the girl splayed against the fence next to the show office. It was not a pretty sight.

"Ring one, all halt, please; ring one, all halt," came the announcement. Although everyone had halted, not everything had halted. The white flash of a pony continued galloping around the ring, seeming more crazed now without its rider. Two of the show officials entered the ring. Showing their years of experience, they slowed the pony, caught its broken bridle, and led it out the gate.

A medical assistant in a white uniform reached the girl, who still bawled in pain. In minutes seeming like hours, another assistant came, and they moved the girl to a stretcher. As they carried her off, a few people clapped, but it was mostly silent.

The class continued. *What?!* Sadie thought. *How could they do that? They don't even know if the girl who fell is all right! This wasn't right.*

"I'm going to go find out if she's okay," Sadie said to Brady.

Brady stood staring into the middle of the ring. "Maybe it's a good idea for me to stay being your groom forever. I'll come with you now."

"No, that's not a good idea," Sadie said. She wasn't sure what she was going to see, but knew for sure she didn't want Brady to see it.

"Why not?"

"Well, because she's a girl, and you're a boy, and they may be doing medical things to her."

"But the guys who carried her off were boys."

Hmmm. He was right.

Amanda interrupted their discourse. "Sadie, time for you and your groom to go tack up. Give yourself extra time so you're not rushing. As soon as this class ends, get on up there, and meet me over at the schooling ring as soon as you are ready. Twenty minutes tops."

From the loudspeaker, "All riders in ring one, line up, please, with your numbers facing the judge."

"But what about...." Amanda strode back to her place at the fence, clipboard in hand, ready to record the placings of her riders.

"In first place, it's Erin Rettig, riding Loftmar's Better Than Ever; in second place, James Wilson riding Billy Walkabout; in third place, Cathi Croson, riding Happy Feet; in fourth place, Virginia Nylin riding Honey Bear; in fifth place, Danielle Needles riding Hamlet's Lady; and in sixth place, Bethany Hernandez riding Ima Custom Fit. Riders, prepare for class 105."

"Woo hoo! I knew we would win," whooped Brady, obviously over his feelings about not being able to go visit the injured girl.

As the riders exited the ring, Erin walked out with the corners of her mouth upturned, appearing relaxed for a minute. Jimmy picked up his ribbon from the ribbon girl and pumped it in the air as if saying "victory," and smiled at the group. Jimmy's dad held his cell phone in the air in return.

Sadie managed, "Congratulations. You guys looked great."

"Of course we did, just like you will. Oh, and of course we can't forget you shared your groom with me. The final touch," Jimmy said.

"I meant your riding looked great. You never looked worried."

"What's there to worry about?"

The girl flying off the horse came to Sadie's mind for one thing.

Amanda reminded, "Sadie, you need to go now. Hurry up. Jimmy and Erin you need to get back in there for your next two classes."

"Okay, sorry. I'm on my way," Sadie said, with a small wave. "Good luck, everyone."

As Sadie traversed the hill to the stalls one more time, it dawned on her. With Jimmy in his classes between now and Sadie's class, how could he help her get ready?

15

A Cry for Help

Sadie heard Lucky's unquestionable whinny. It sounded more like a panicked cry.

"C'mon, something's wrong." She tapped Brady and jogged the rest of the way to the barn, hearing Lucky's cries louder and more distinct as they came closer.

She saw Lucky's coat soaked in sweat. He pawed his stall door, frantic, threw his head, and cried more. "What's wrong, boy?" Sadie pleaded, trying to calm her distraught horse. She opened the stall door, and Lucky almost ran her down trying to get past her. Fortunately, she closed the door in time to keep him in and stroked his neck. But her efforts to calm him weren't working.

Brady reached in the treat bucket, grabbed a piece of carrot, and opened his hand to give it to Lucky, just like Sadie had taught him. That made Lucky stop crying. At least while he chewed. And now Lucky was pacing, with Sadie in his stall.

"Please hand me his currycomb," Sadie directed. "He's been sweating so much, his coat is a mess. I don't know what's wrong, or how long he's been like this."

Sadie felt terrible. This whole show she'd been so self-absorbed. She hadn't been concerned about Lucky. After all, this was his first show, too. And something bothered him. But how strange, he had been fine just before they left for Jimmy and Erin's classes. The worst thoughts came into Sadie's mind. Maybe someone poisoned him. Or maybe the commotion upset him so much he was colicking, the most common horse killer sickness often brought on by stress.

"Well, what do we have here? This isn't the Lucky I know."

"Austin! Thank God you are here. I've never been so happy to see you. Come help me, please."

Austin stroked Lucky's nose, and Lucky calmed. Austin always had that effect on Lucky, and on everyone, including Sadie. "What's up, boy? Too much excitement for you here?" Austin kept stroking the horse's nose, and moved to his neck. Lucky turned his neck and leaned into Austin's scratch, quiet for the first time since Sadie returned.

"I don't know what's happening." Sadie's speech picked up pace and her voice got higher with each word. "He's pacing, and crazy, and nervous, and it's awful. I'm so worried, and I don't know what to do."

"The first thing you need to do is calm down. It doesn't help him if you're crazy like this. He senses it. So take a few deep breaths and try to relax. Why are you so nervous — never mind — I don't need you to talk about it and get him more excited. Just try to relax."

"Hi, Austin," Brady chimed in. "I'm here to help,

too. Earlier I helped Sadie not be nervous, but then I found I wasn't much help when Lucky got nervous."

"You've been a great help, I'm sure. Can you imagine if Sadie had found Lucky like this by herself? I don't even want to think about it," Austin said, pretending to shiver.

Entering Lucky's stall, Austin continued petting him and speaking to him in calming tones. Lucky started to drop his head, a sign of contentment. "So what happened?"

"I don't know!"

"Okay, start telling me what's happened since the last time you saw Lucky," Austin said.

"Well, Brady and I helped Jimmy get Billy ready for his classes, which he's in now. And then Jimmy, Billy, Erin, and Everett, Brady, and I, all went down to the rings so they could school and start their classes. And when Brady and I came back, we found Lucky like this." She sighed, but tried to seem calm for Lucky's sake.

"So let me say this back to you. Lucky was here, with all the other horses, including the one he lives next-door to at Loftmar, and the next thing, everybody's gone. Horses and humans. In a strange place."

The light bulb went on. How could Sadie have been so stupid! Lucky felt abandoned by his herd. When Sadie and Brady left the first time, Mom stayed with Lucky. The other horses were with him, except for Snickers, whose stall was so far away Lucky probably didn't notice. It made sense. Leave it to Austin, the non-horse guy, to figure out the problem.

"He seems to be happier now with his human herd returned. Let's keep him busy, and distracted," Austin continued.

"Okay, but we need to get Sadie ready for her class, too. Here's Lucky's bridle," Brady offered, handing Austin Lucky's leather bridle for the horse's head.

"Thank you, buddy. Can you hand me the hard brush? And are you Sadie's groom?"

"Well yes, I am. Can't you tell? And I was thinking about maybe showing, but then I saw something that made me think maybe I'll just be a groom for a while."

"Really, what was that?" Austin asked.

Brady shook his head at Austin, who caught his drift.

Sadie said, "The sooner we get Lucky where the other horses are, the better off he'll be. Even if it means he's not spotless. Right now, I need to think about Lucky." *Rather than myself for a change.*

"Agreed." Austin smoothed Lucky's coat with his hand, and asked Brady to hand him the saddle. The three worked in unison getting tack to stall and tack in place. As Sadie exited the stall, her mom and Jessica arrived.

"We're here to help. But it doesn't appear you need help. Why are you ready so early?" Jessica queried.

"We need to get Lucky down there. I can explain on the way. But can someone make sure my hair is in my helmet right and my number isn't on upside down or something." Sadie felt better already.

Jessica and Sadie's mom helped Sadie with her coat, tie, hair, helmet, and number in record time, while the boys kept Lucky busy.

A few steps down the hill, Lucky started to cry again. Oh no. Things were going so well. But Sadie refused to get flustered. She kept marching forward and stroked Lucky's neck, letting him know everything was going to be all right. Finally, she heard Billy's answer to Lucky's call in the distance, and she thought she saw Lucky smile. "That's better, huh, boy? No, your friends didn't leave you here. Let's go see them."

Jimmy and Erin's last class looked half over, but Lucky's demeanor changed in the other horses' presence. Sadie had walked Lucky to the rings earlier, so these were not new sights to him. He didn't usually react poorly to new situations and was not "spooky" by nature, so she had that on her side. Lucky normally took things in stride, which is why this latest situation confounded Sadie. She learned a lot before her first class even began.

Sadie hopped on Lucky and walked him around the grounds, all within sight and earshot of his buddies. He felt tense, which made Sadie more tense. Sadie calmed herself formulating good thoughts, remembering how nice and easy Jessica, Erin, and Jimmy made it look. Austin joined Sadie walking Lucky along the ringside grass pasture.

"Sadie, you need to relax. Remember, this isn't about you. As I recall, you wanted to do this for Dad, and he cheered you on in an e-mail this morning. And if Dad were here, what would he say?"

"Trraannnqquuiillloo," they both said slow and low in unison. That was Dad's Spanish version of "chill." The tension left Sadie's body and mind for a moment.

Jimmy and Erin's final class ended, and they each won ribbons again, in the same order. From across the ring, Amanda motioned Sadie to move to the schooling ring, which she did with Austin by her side. Lucky started getting antsy as soon as they moved away from his horse friends, who headed back to the barn. He cried and whinnied again, and started to sound the same as he did a half hour ago. All that calming for nothing!

Brady watched this from a distance, and then bolted up the hill. Sadie would have told him not to run around horses, in his continuing education, but he wouldn't have heard her at that distance. And right now, she couldn't train Brady; she needed to get Lucky back under control.

They entered the schooling ring, and Lucky trotted sideways, although she only asked him to walk. He tossed his head, cried pitiful sounds, and arched his neck so high he looked like a Halloween cat. Sadie tried to remain calm, but Lucky's behavior didn't go unnoticed by the other horses and riders in the ring.

"Keep walking him, Sadie. That's right, and lower your hands. That's better. Make a small circle, and give yourself room. You're fine," Amanda coached from the center of the schooling ring.

She was not fine. Her horse was about to explode from underneath her. Couldn't her coach see that?

"All entries for class number 107, please report to ring one; class 107, ring one," came the familiar loudspeaker voice.

"Okay, Sadie, let's go. I'll walk and talk with you. Yes, Lucky is excited, but that's to be expected at his first show. Just breathe, talk to him, and keep nice quiet hands. You'll do fine. Keep away from the other horses, got it?"

"Are you…I mean, are you sure this is going to be okay?" Sadie's voice quivered.

"I wouldn't put you in danger. Now remember why you are here — to have fun. Now, go get 'em, and Lucky, you take care of her."

Sadie realized she needed to rethink her ideas of fun. And really, she wasn't here to have fun anyway. Maybe other people were, but she wasn't. She was here for Dad. She would have to pull this off for him.

16

The Big Test

"Good luck," Mom wished, smiling and acting as if everything was normal when Sadie entered the ring,

Sadie gulped air, trying to breathe, and found a spot on the rail a good distance from the other horses. Lucky continued to cry, the only horse doing so. The announcer hadn't started the class yet, so Sadie hoped the judge wouldn't hold the current activity against her. Even though it was her first show, Sadie knew enough to know the horse was supposed to appear calm and pleasurable, not like a wild mustang in a pen for the first time in its life.

Austin stood by the bleachers, and pointed his phone's camera in her direction. He took the camera away from his eye, cupped his other hand around his mouth and shouted "I believe!" Sadie wanted to cry. Leave it to her brother to remind her of the special saying she used with Lucky that always made things better. Shutting out everything around her, she thought as hard as she could, *I believe, I believe, I believe.* It didn't work. Then, she remembered Amanda's words, "talk to him." She whispered to Lucky, "I believe, I believe, I believe," in cadence with his steps. She couldn't believe it was working.

Whew, Sadie realized. Maybe I *can* do this. The official class hadn't started yet, so she still had time to continue working the magic.

Sadie added another phrase, to help remind her, "This is for Dad, Lucky, this is for Dad." A few more deep breaths, and she started the sequence again. She scratched Lucky's withers in front of his saddle using the hand out of the judge's view, as if to say, "Yes, Lucky, this is better." A few steps later, she repeated the sequence: "I believe, I believe, I believe," step, step, step, step. "This is for Dad, Lucky, this is for Dad."

"Who are you talking to?" sounded a voice from a horse way too close behind her. She didn't need to look. She knew who it was.

Rachel sidled up to Sadie on the inside of the ring, too close for comfort, on a large almost-black thoroughbred. Sadie turned to face the penetrating eyes and managed, "Lucky. This is my horse, Lucky. And he likes me to talk to him."

"Well, that's stupid, but if the judge sees it, then good for me!"

Why does this girl taunt me? But Sadie answered back, not quite sure why, "My coach told me it was okay."

"Another reason why I don't have a coach. They don't know what they are doing. But if you believe her, well...ta ta," and off she went, cutting across the ring. Thank goodness.

Sadie believed her coach. Amanda rode in big shows for years, and in the short time she'd been working with her, Sadie's riding improved. Besides, Amanda's prescription for Lucky's problem worked. How could she not believe her?

"Class number 107, you are being judged at a walk." The words she'd been waiting for since entering the ring. Okay, Lucky, showtime.

Just in case Rachel was right, Sadie decided to think her series of thoughts rather than say them. So far, so good. When she rounded the bend to where the Loftmar crowd stood, she caught Brady wildly waving his hands. He pointed to Billy, who Jimmy held with a lead rope. Her little groom who knew nothing about horses thought to run up and get Billy because Lucky needed him.

Lucky pointed his head in Billy's direction, and the older, wiser Billy gave Lucky a knowing nod. Sadie smiled, and didn't care at that point whether the judge would be mad or not. She loved what happened. And apparently, Lucky did, too. She knew Dad would approve.

"Smile for the camera," Austin directed, as she passed him. He didn't need to say it because Sadie hadn't stopped smiling since Lucky had calmed down.

"Ring one, all trot; ring one, all trot."

Sadie gently squeezed her legs, and Lucky barely moved. She squeezed again, and he started backing. Then, he tried to turn to the inside of the ring, out of nowhere. Sadie got him back under control, and spoke to him again: "Remember, Lucky, this is for Dad." She finally got Lucky moving forward when another competitor passed him, but it still was barely a trot.

Sadie and Lucky managed to make it to the top of the ring, with another two riders passing them. Then, Lucky shot off in a fast working trot. Sadie pulled him back, and he tossed his head. This was so unlike him.

"C'mon now, easy." That wasn't working. They continued at the bullet-paced trot, now passing other riders, until Lucky got to the bottom of the ring. And he slowed. A lot.

Sadie realized what was happening. Lucky slowed when leaving Billy, and sped up when seeing him again. Think fast. Well, with what he had just done, they weren't going to win this class, so let's at least try to make it less stressful for Lucky. As soon as Lucky got through the bottom part of the large oval arena, Sadie used her left rein to move Lucky's head to the inside of the arena. He could see Billy again. Not fine equitation riding, but she needed to keep Lucky sane. It was the best she could think of at the time.

As Lucky seemed happier, Sadie chanted a ditty she made up on the spot. "I believe, I believe, I believe, we will, will, will see Billy again." It made her chuckle, and she noticed Lucky felt her release of laughter in his gait. He kept a normal pace this time heading toward his buddy. The judge in the center of the huge ring couldn't hear her, but may see her lips moving. Sadie considered her choices at the time — look better, or help Lucky. She decided to help Lucky.

"Ring one, reverse directions, please; ring one, reverse directions."

Sadie repeated her routine in the opposite direction, and while the minutes passed, Lucky's mood improved. When the announcer asked riders to line up in the center, meaning the class was over, Sadie silently cried *hallelujah*. Standing in the center of the ring, facing her Loftmar team, she patted Lucky's neck again and told him he'd been a good boy. She had to remember, Lucky had to be the youngest horse in the ring.

The announcer called the placings, and Sadie wasn't surprised she didn't earn a ribbon. She heard Rachel's name: fourth place, and her horse's name, Black Widow. Sadie thought that was an awful name for a lovely mare. They placed up to sixth place, so Sadie thought, maybe she was seventh. It could have been close. With everything happening, she surprised herself by even thinking this. And she knew she'd do better next time.

In the moments before the next class, Rachel approached Sadie riding too close again and said, "I can fix that horse for you, you know. And not by talking to him. Give me the chance, and I'll show you."

"Um, okay...thanks, sure," Sadie answered, not understanding what she meant and why, and not wanting to spend another minute thinking about it.

The next class was far less eventful for Sadie and Lucky, and was still only a walk/trot class. Lucky realized Billy would not be going away, and started to warm up to being in the show ring. Sadie wasn't sure if it was Lucky's assimilation to his surroundings or her own taste of competition that earned them their first ribbon of the day. But the pink fifth place ribbon shone a bright blue first place in Sadie's eyes.

Sadie's nerves built up for her final class, where she would canter. Lucky had a beautiful canter...when he wanted to canter. But as a young horse, his stubborn tendencies regularly surfaced, and he had never cantered with this many horses in the ring at one time. Lucky's 1200-pound body mismatched Sadie's 110-pound frame by far, and she admitted she was unsure about this. But, she took her place on the rail and hoped for the best. And she wished away the flashback of the recent white pony incident.

Just before the class began, Sadie recognized the almond eyes and light brown skin of the girl she cheered on this morning who rode the gray mare. Standing at the rail, the girl said, "Make it easy!" and smiled. Sadie was touched because this stranger cared enough to find her after her classes to return the favor. She already felt better.

Much to Sadie's surprise, their final class turned out to be their best of the day. Lucky performed perfect canter transitions in both directions and listened to everything Sadie told him to do. He made it look easy, and the judge rewarded them. Sadie and Lucky earned a spectacular red ribbon — second place. And for the first time of the day, they beat Rachel and Black Widow. Sadie wanted to burst with excitement, pride, or she didn't know what. They had done it — second place!

Sadie exited the arena after her final class and dismounted, greeted by a cheering group of Loftmar friends and her family.

"Dad will be so proud of you! I took a video to show him with you cantering. And then they announced the ribbons, so he'll hear it, too. I'll send it now — real-time. What a great job!" Austin gave her a tight hug. Most sixteen-year-old brothers wouldn't do that, but she was glad she had the one who would.

"I knew you could do it," Amanda said. "Good job."

Rachel brushed by them, and didn't look back. Jimmy looked at Sadie, shrugged his shoulders, and shook his head. Sadie let Lucky bump noses with Billy, a friendly horse hello.

"Let's get these guys back to their stalls and get them water. We've had enough excitement for a while," Jimmy said, walking toward the stables with Billy.

"C'mon, Brady, you've got work to do." Sadie followed.

The girl with the almond eyes caught up to Sadie, and walked beside her. "Hi, I see you have quite a fan club," she joked, in her delicate voice. "Lucky you. My name is Fay, and I wanted to say hi, and to thank you for your encouragement this morning."

"Hi, Fay. This isn't my fan club, it's just people from my barn, and my family, well, and my neighbor. Okay, you are right, I am lucky," Sadie replied. "I've never met a Fay before."

"Really? Come to think of it, I've never met a Sadie either."

"Look at how much we already have in common," Sadie said.

"In Tagalog, my name means 'faith.' My mom is Filipina, and she named me. It should be spelled F-E, but she said people would always pronounce it wrong if she spelled it the right way."

"That's neat." Sadie wondered what her name meant.

"Anyhow, I have to go now. But I wanted to say hi and thank you in person for reaching out this morning. I guess it was pretty obvious how scared I was. You helped me, and I appreciate that."

"Oh, it was nothing. And hey, you came back to help me, too. That was nice of you." Sadie reached up and patted Lucky's neck. "And Lucky appreciated it, too."

"I can tell," Fay said, smiling, and touching him gently. "Very pretty horse, Sadie."

"Thank you. Your gray is pretty, too. Are you showing the rest of the shows this year?"

Fay rolled her eyes and said, "Yes, unfortunately. I've been showing a few years, and I still get so nervous. I keep waiting for the day that it will be, well, easy, as you say, and I'm not there yet."

"Maybe this will be the year," Sadie said, as if she had been showing for a decade.

"Maybe it will. Nice meeting you, Sadie, and see you next time. Bye, Lucky!" Sadie's new friend departed.

Sadie survived her first show. And they improved in every class. By the grand finale, she would make Dad so proud.

17

Attention to Detail

Mom drove Sadie to her second trip to the Caisson Platoon Equine Assisted Programs today at Fort Belvoir military base also in the neighboring state of Virginia. Sadie looked forward to the time spent with her mom in the car where just the two of them could talk. She wasn't ready to talk about her fears about Dad or working with the veterans, but she had other things on her mind. Many times Mom helped her make sense out of her crazy Sadie thoughts.

"Mom, why do I find myself trying to be nice to that awful girl Rachel, who has been nasty to me every time I've seen her?"

"Maybe you've spent so much time with the horses, you've picked up their habits. You know — like how they sense things in people."

"You mean like how Lucky knows when I'm having a bad day, and how he really likes certain people, like you, even though you're not a horse person."

"Something like that. Maybe you sense something in that girl — somehow she needs your help. Well, it's my theory. Or you are being who you are — trying to look out for people's feelings and being compassionate."

"Hmmm...maybe it's instinct — kind of funny when you think about it. Again, a lot like horses," Sadie considered.

"You've always been sensitive and kind, Sadie; it's one of the reasons you are here today. Keep following your instincts. You can't go wrong being kind to people, even if they are unkind people themselves. And thank you for talking to me. I didn't realize that girl bothered you so much."

"I try not to let things get to me. But since we had time, I at least wanted your opinion. Since you're working as an intelligence officer I figure you solve problems all the time, so this one would be easy for you. And I was right." Sadie smiled at her mom.

During the rest of the ride, Sadie told her mom everything she could remember about the Caisson Platoon Equine Assisted Programs, and Mom seemed interested. Sadie helped navigate to the facility once they arrived on the military base. When they approached the barn, an older gentlemen greeted them.

"May I help you, ma'am?" a white-haired man with bright blue eyes behind his spectacles asked Sadie's mom. Sadie guessed he was about Grandma Collins' age. But he stood tall, and his body reminded her of a professional football player.

"I hope so," Sadie's mom answered. "I'm Liz Navarro, and this is my daughter, Sadie. We're here to meet a Captain John Vinson; Sadie will be helping him today. Sadie's a volunteer," Mom said, matching the man's proud, erect posture.

"Good, because I'm Captain John Vinson, and I need all the help I can get," he joked. "It's great to meet you both. I knew you were coming, Sadie, and I looked forward to meeting you. You're ready to work, aren't you?"

"Oh yes, Sir! And I have a horse, so I know what to do around horses."

"Glad to hear it. Mrs. Beckman spoke highly of you." He turned to Sadie's mom. "You must be very proud, ma'am."

"Oh, I am. Believe me. And Captain, are you a Navy captain?"

"Well, I'm a retired Navy captain now. I understand Sadie's father is in the Navy."

"Yes, he is," Mom answered. "He's in Afghanistan now, but we're looking forward to having him home very soon."

"My mom's in the Navy, too, Captain — sort of," Sadie piped in, her chance to be proud. "She's a civilian, but she works at the Office of Naval Intelligence. And she can't talk about it much."

Captain Vinson looked at Sadie, and then her mom, then back to Sadie. "That's interesting, because I worked in that field also."

"Really!" Sadie couldn't hide her interest. "How cool. Can you tell me the things Mom won't?"

"You wouldn't want to get us in trouble now, would you?" the raspy-voiced captain asked. Sadie could tell her mom liked him.

"I'd better go so you two can get to work," Sadie's mom said. "I'll go wait in the car; I have plenty to do."

"Ma'am, help yourself to our offices here, or there's nice areas outside the barn. Wherever you are most comfortable, please make yourself at home."

"Thank you, Captain. I'll stay out of the way. This is Sadie's project, and I want her to get the most out of her limited time here. When should I come back?"

"For this session, two hours. I'll keep an eye out for you and bring her back in your direction when we're done. How's that?"

"Thank you. And thank you again for your service, and what you are doing here today."

The burly captain nodded, and Sadie could tell he was embarrassed. He mumbled, "You're welcome. C'mon, Sadie, work to do," and he ambled off toward another spotless tack room.

Captain Vinson explained the process for cleaning the Caisson Platoon tack and showed her where every sponge, brush, and tool she'd need resided. He reminded her that every piece of equipment had its place and to remember to put each back in its place.

"One of the reasons everything looks so neat and orderly here is because everyone follows the rules. And we don't cut corners. I'm sure your dad, being a Navy man, has explained to you the importance of attention to detail."

"He has," Sadie answered. "But honestly, I don't remember exactly what it means."

He placed a large leather saddle on a saddle rack in front of Sadie, and one in front of himself, and a cleaning box between the two of them. "Here, we can talk while we're working. When I was a boss, people considered me a tough guy. And I was. But it was because I'd seen firsthand the difference one word can make. So when I heard someone describe an enemy ship as near one place, and I knew it was near another, I couldn't let it go. It makes a big difference. Let me show you an example of what this can mean with tack."

He reached over and unfastened the back side of the stirrup strap on the saddle Sadie cleaned. He placed the flap back down where it belonged, covering the stirrup strap. "Watch." He pushed down on the stirrup, which came loose on the strap and dangled toward the ground because it wasn't buckled. Sadie retrieved the loose stirrup, returning it to the Captain, meeting his eyes.

"This one simple action makes the difference of whether a student leaves today making a positive step ahead, or falling off, feeling a sense of failure, and never returning again. That's why I've always been a stickler for attention to detail. It's important in everything you do, no matter how mundane the task might seem. This was reinforced more times than I can count in my career."

He paused. "If I can teach you one thing, here's my contribution: remember attention to detail."

"Consider it done," Sadie said. She felt so comfortable with this gruff old guy who seemed to be such a contradiction. For a minute, she even contemplated telling him her fears about working with the veterans, but decided against it. If she couldn't tell Austin, Mr. Edwards, or her mom, why would she want to tell this person who had been a stranger fifteen minutes ago?

"Do you have any questions about our program?" the Captain asked, while working on the cantle of his saddle with a toothbrush and a toothpick to remove the specks of dirt.

"I want to know more about post-traumatic stress disorder."

"That's an interesting request. Why do you ask about PTSD? Are you worried about your dad?"

"No, my dad's not even back yet, and I'm not a psychiatrist or anything. But in our 'discussions,'" she said, putting her two fingers in the air around the word as if putting them in quote marks, "he seems like normal Dad. Except he used to write more."

"That's common. As time goes on, people tend to miss home more, and writing makes them miss home even more. Sometimes it's easier to stay busy and distracted rather than think about things that make you sad."

Kind of like me and my horse showing and volunteer work, Sadie reflected.

"So, is PTSD part of your studies, or is this to help you better understand some of our participants?" Captain Vinson asked.

"A bit of both. I read a lot, and I admit I have worried about it and my dad. My grandma told me that my grandpa suffered from PTSD until the day he died. But in those days, no one talked about it."

"Your grandma is right. Fortunately, we've come a long way. And it takes brave people to confront this disorder. We're lucky to have programs like this one that spend time and research to help people with not just physical ailments, but mental and emotional ones. People respond to different therapies, and equine therapy is proving itself in many ways every day." He pointed to a section on Sadie's saddle where she missed a spot. "Tell me more about your grandpa."

"My grandpa, or 'Pop Pop' as we used to call him, because our oldest cousin couldn't say 'grandpa' when she was young, was funny, and we all loved him. His eyes sparkled, and they were bright, bright blue." Sadie looked down to make sure she continued cleaning tack while talking, remembering she was here to work. "He read books all the time, and I got that trait from him. Grandma Collins said he read a full paperback book every day after he retired. He was super skinny, and even though he was ten years older than my grandma, he looked way older than that. He shuffled when he walked, and when he wasn't being funny, he looked very sad. And none of the cousins knew why."

"Go on. And here's a black bridle to clean. This saddle isn't going to get any cleaner," he said, winking at her and switching Sadie's spotless tack with a matching bridle.

"I feel terrible," Sadie almost whispered. "He used to tell us war stories, and we thought they were boring. Maybe he needed to tell someone. And we hardly listened."

"Don't feel bad, Sadie. You were kids. How old were you?"

"Let's see...Pop Pop died when our family was in Spain, and I was ten. So it was before that time. And my oldest cousin, Michele, is two years older than me – so when he was telling us stories, the oldest of us was ten. Why?"

"Think. You're a smart girl — look at the fancy math you just did," he said, grinning again.

"What does math have to do with it? Oh...I see. How could a bunch of kids between the ages of two and ten have solved his problems?"

"I'm not saying it wasn't nice not to listen to your grandpa. But I hope you're not somehow blaming yourself for something you could not have known how to help."

"I didn't say we didn't listen; we did. We'd just

talk later about how boring it was. Well, and sometimes we tried to change the subject. Boy, I wish I could go back and listen now."

"You don't have to go back. Sounds like you learned something on your own. I bet you'll listen to someone else in the future. Okay, time to move on. We have horses to groom, too."

They moved to the barn, and the Captain brought out a giant gray Percheron horse named Omaha. "Many of the horses here are in training. They are not as used to standing still as those at Fort Myer. But they are good soldiers, and they are learning. And you can help by being consistent with them while we're grooming. Stay nice and gentle, and correct them when they move around," he continued. He hooked up the horse's halter to the cross ties to keep him in place in the grooming station.

Sadie began currying the big draft horse. She was glad she was tall enough now to reach the massive horse's back without having to ask for help from her supervisor. She hesitated, but asked anyway. "Captain, can you tell me about you?"

"Well, I don't like to talk much about myself, but I also don't work with young girls much. And since you've been so open with me, I'll share a bit. But I can't let you do all the work, let me help."

"Thank you. I don't mean to be nosy, and my mom would kill me if she knew I asked. But I feel I have a lot to learn from you, so I'd like to know more. You know, for my school project," Sadie said.

"Since you asked, I began my service in the Vietnam War. And although in the Navy, I spent a lot of time doing ground stuff. It used to be top secret, but now it's in the front pages of the newspapers and in books. Good people helped me through my physical problems. And I remember how people treated my friends when they returned, which is another reason I volunteer here now. I want to give back and help people understand they are valued."

"I didn't suffer from PTSD, but I changed. People change in life, and not just because of war. I saw this in life before the military, and over and over again during the thirty-one years I served. We can't expect people to stay the same forever; we need to respect those changes."

They talked more, groomed more, and before Sadie knew it, two hours sped by. As she and her new friend were leaving, a bus pulled up with today's students. Sadie froze. Captain Vinson patted her on the back, turned and waved at the incoming troops. "Smile and wave, Sadie. Don't worry; they're not going to hurt you. They want to be treated as normal. You're here to help them, remember?"

Sadie stared at the bus, and waved a small wave. She looked to the Captain seeking his permission to go to her mom's car. No permission granted.

"You know more about the horses than you do about these people. But from the short time we've spent together, I can tell you care about people. Everyone here has something making them different than they used to be. Some of them have held their problems in longer than others, like the folks from my era.

"But in the end, for the most part, no one wants special favors. These folks just want people like you and me to see them for the people they are, not for their diagnoses or their injuries. They accept you, so think how easy it is for you to accept them. Next time, I'll introduce you to a few folks, and you'll see what I mean. Take care now."

Sadie turned to leave, heart racing. She had been looking forward to coming back, cleaning more tack, brushing more horses, and getting her own form of therapy by learning from this wise old man. But she realized he was right. Sadie needed to conquer her fears and start dealing with all kinds of people, even those she feared, if she truly wanted to work in equine therapy.

She needed to find strength. And she had one week to do it.

18

At the Second Show

Sadie felt a new confidence going into her second horse show. She learned lessons from the first show and participated in more group lessons getting Lucky used to the horse crowds. She understood the routine and what to expect, so it would not be as daunting to her as the first time. Plus, her trusty groom accompanied her, chasing those pesky stomach butterflies and bees away.

Brady rode with Sadie and in her mom's car today. Sadie had begged her mom not to make Brady's dad mad by telling him he was irresponsible for leaving Brady at the equestrian center on his own after the last show. Her mom said she had to mention it, Brady's dad being new to Maryland. When Mom returned from speaking with her new next-door neighbor, she slammed the door, and her words were short: "Brady will come with us from now on. That's that."

Sadie hadn't pressed her mom for details.

Mom dropped off Sadie and Brady at Lucky's stall nestled among the other Loftmar horses. Together they brushed Lucky in his stall, while Mom went to go finish off the administrative show details with Coach Amanda. The grooming twosome chatted about the swirls in Lucky's coat and how happy he seemed today. They agreed the weather would be better without the gray skies and hint of rain to come, but vowed not to let it get to them. They also concluded since Sadie was no longer nervous, neither was Lucky.

And Sadie wished she believed that part.

"Where's the groom?" Austin asked, peering into Lucky's stall, smiling.

"Austin!" Brady shouted, looking up to Austin like the big brother he never had. And Austin treated Brady like the special kid he was. "I'm right here."

"Good, because I have something for you."

"For me?" Brady asked, head cocked.

"You're the groom, aren't you?" Austin asked, presenting a navy-blue ball cap with "GROOM" embroidered in gold across the front.

"No! This can't be. Oh my. No one's ever done something like this for me. Oh, Austin, I promise I'll take care of your hat."

"It's not my hat, kid, it's yours. Katie and I had it made for you. We figured people should know who you are, right? But you can keep your old one instead if you like…."

"No — no, not at all. I'm just…well, sorry…I just don't know what to say."

Sadie looked lovingly at her brother, and then at the beaming Brady, and told him, "I think all you need to do is say 'thank you,' Brady."

Austin reached over the stall door and handed Brady the new hat, which he handled like a king's crown. He admired it from every angle, then removed his fisherman's cap with one hand, resting it on the stall door. With both hands, Brady placed his new hat on his head, adjusting the bill to the perfect angle. "Thank you," he said, looking at his feet and still not seeming to know how to react.

"Did you see the back?" Katie asked, quiet up to this point. "Take a look."

Brady removed the hat and flipped it the opposite direction. On the back above the keyhole, he read "BRADY." He looked at Katie, and whispered, "Thank you, too."

"Oh, it was nothing," Katie said, chipper as always. "We're glad you appreciate it. We'll let you all get back to your work now, okay?"

"Katie...you can have my old hat...that is...if you want it," Brady spurted out.

"Awww, thanks, Brady," Katie said, lifting the tattered cap from the stall door. "If it rains today, this will help keep my hair dry and the rain out of my eyes. How thoughtful of you." Katie plopped the hat that always looked silly on Brady onto her own head. Of course, she looked like a fashion model.

Austin turned to Katie and said, "I hope no one mistakes you for a groom now, because I know you don't know the first thing to do."

"No, but *you* do," she laughed, and looped her arm through her boyfriend's, walking off toward the arenas.

Okay, so maybe Katie-bug did mean well. And if she made the people Sadie cared for happy, maybe Sadie could be happy for that. Sometimes Sadie scared herself when she had these revelations.

The first few classes and divisions rolled by without drama, and Jessica scored well again. And this time, Sadie planned to have Lucky by the arena ready for his next classes while Billy competed in his classes. That way, Lucky would not be distraught when Billy disappeared, like the last time. Jimmy agreed to keep Billy nearby during Lucky's classes. Even though this wasn't a team sport, the Loftmar riders wanted each other to succeed. In secret, Sadie hoped Jimmy agreed to do this not just because she was with the same barn, but because he wanted to do it for her.

Standing outside the ring during Jimmy and Erin's class, Sadie told Brady to pose holding Lucky's reins, so she could get a picture of him at work. Brady smiled, pointed to the title on his hat, and said, "Grrrooommm," mocking how most people say, "Cheeeesse." Sadie laughed because the words "groom" and "cheese" didn't create the same facial expression. He looked more like he was puckering up.

"What a dork," Sadie heard behind her. She didn't have to look. Rachel.

Katie shouted from the fence line, where she'd been watching the show. "Hey, Sadie, let's get a picture together." She grabbed Austin's hand and brought him over to where Lucky, Sadie, and Brady stood. In seconds, Katie arranged the group, fussing over Brady, and took her phone out of her pocket. She whirled to face the girl closest to them and asked, "Would you mind?" head tilted, smiling.

Sadie cringed. Katie had no idea who Rachel was. Sadie still hadn't gotten over the fact the person getting ready to take their picture just called her friend a dork.

"I'd be happy to," Rachel sneered. "Nice hat, by the way." Sadie remembered Rachel making fun of Brady's hat a month ago. What a hypocrite. Oh, or perhaps that was her point — making fun of Katie. Rachel half-heartedly pointed the camera phone in their direction and clicked the button. "There."

Katie, oblivious, said, "Thank you!" taking the phone back to check the picture. "Look, Austin, you're smiling!" Katie seemed delighted.

"Austin…oh, yes, now I remember you. I was trying to figure out how I knew you," Rachel purred. "But I didn't recognize the little blonde girl. Now I know, from last summer…same cowboy hat…from California."

"Um, yeah, I remember. C'mon, Kates, let's go," Austin said, walking back toward the rail, as if he cared what happened in the ring. Sadie saw that he wanted to get away from this person who radiated bad vibes.

"What's the rush? We can get acquainted again…I mean, it's been so long," Rachel continued, suggesting she'd known Austin better than the ten minutes they spent at Connor's Horse Farm last summer.

Katie flashed a look at Austin, not understanding. "Well, you can stay and catch up if you want, but I want to go see Erin and Jimmy win their ribbons. This is my first horse show! See you later, and thanks for the picture, guys." Katie started back toward the fence.

"Cheerleader?" Rachel asked, looking down her nose over the top of her tacky sunglasses not necessary on such a gloomy day.

"No, track and field, and my girlfriend. Speaking of, gotta run now," Austin said, tipping his cowboy hat, and jogging off to follow his girl.

Turning to Sadie, Rachel said, "Such a shame.

Well, there's always that other boy at your barn, Timmy, right?"

"His name is Jimmy," Sadie fumed, wondering why she was helping this chameleon.

"That's right. Guess I'd better catch him before the end of the day. I see him all the time at school now. He wants me to ride with him. But can you blame him? You wouldn't mind, would you?" she laughed, tossing her cascade of black hair back, posing again.

"Um, no, I guess not." *Why should she care? It's not that obvious, is it? Is it the way she looks at him?* Trying to be nice, Sadie continued, "So, you don't believe in coaches. But does anyone come with you here — parents, friends, or people from Connor's Horse Farm?" *That's it,* Sadie analyzed, *she's mean because she's lonely.*

"We're not one of those goofy show barns wearing matching clothes and all that nonsense. I pay one of the other girls to share the horse trailer ride over, but we're not friends. She's just a horse taxi to me."

"And your parents?" Sadie couldn't fathom why she cared, but she asked anyway.

"Look, I'm sixteen, not a baby anymore. I don't need my mommy and daddy to hold my hand, clap, and take pictures anymore. You'll grow out of it, too."

This tortured Sadie. She wanted her dad here more than anything else, and the closest thing she had to it was an e-mail that she kept in her pocket, wishing her a good second show. Here this girl didn't even want her parents near her. How sad. Sadie wondered if she would grow out of her current feelings. She hoped not.

"Sadie!" Coach Amanda called. "Time to mount up, now — meet me over in the schooling area in a few."

"Oh dear, that's your coach barking at you. And

she's even right this time. I'd better go get Widow now, too. Meet you in the ring again — toodles."

Toodles? Sadie walked with Brady to the mounting block trying to forget the past five minutes. After she mounted, Brady asked her to stop. He reached with his rag to dust the dirt off Sadie's tall black boot, looking up at her. Pointing to his hat, he said, with a nod, "My new hat is going to bring us luck today."

Sadie nodded back, happy that young Brady hadn't heard the wicked girl's hurtful remark about him. Sadie now needed to perform her absolute best to show Rachel what dork's friends can do.

19

Take Two - In the Ring

"There you go, pull his head in toward the center a hair; there you go, now he's listening. Use that inside rein and inside leg…perfect," Amanda coached while Sadie warmed up Lucky.

He appeared distracted, but so far behaved one hundred times better than he had the last schooling session. Sadie concentrated on staying away from the other riders in the practice ring and thought to herself, *I believe, I believe, I believe.* She still couldn't believe that stupid girl called Brady a name, insulted her brother's girlfriend, flirted with Austin, and suggested Jimmy liked her — all in five minutes. The nerve.

"Sadie! Did you hear me? I said, now let's canter. Ready, when you get to the corner here, pick up your left lead canter," Amanda called, bringing Sadie out of her thoughts.

"Woof, woof," came the sound from her left, as

Rachel passed her while trotting.

"And can*ter*," her coach ordered, emphasizing the last syllable the way they did to help the horse understand the tone.

Sadie sunk into her heels and urged Lucky on, repeating the command to him. Lucky eased into the canter with a rocking horse beat and kept the nice, smooth rhythm they practiced so much at home. Sadie navigated him around horses, and he remained calm. Things were looking good.

"Come over here, and let's talk," Amanda hollered.

What? She couldn't have done it any better. Was it her imagination? But Sadie obeyed, and met Amanda in the center of the ring while the other riders continued schooling. She felt as if she was being scolded in public.

"That was beautiful, Sadie! Ride like that when you get in the ring. You've never looked better. Now let's repeat it in the opposite direction, and we'll be done schooling."

Okay, so Sadie overreacted. Nerves. Or the "woof." Or something. Now she had to remember what she did to make Lucky go so well. Repeat performance.

They cantered on the right lead with the same success, and Sadie slowed Lucky to a walk to cool him. She gave him a big pat on his neck, reassuring him he'd done the right thing. Lucky hadn't cried out, and she was thankful that she spied Billy out of the corner of her eye. Sadie understood horses' great sense of smell. Even if he couldn't see Billy the entire time, he could smell him. The last time, Lucky had been so rattled his senses weren't working right. Or that's what Sadie figured.

"Entries for class 107, please enter ring one now.

Class 107, ring one," sounded the announcer's voice.

Sadie counted more people in this class than the last time. No problem, she felt better prepared. Today the Lucky she bonded with at home had returned. Sadie thought ahead and realized Jimmy and Billy couldn't accompany Lucky to every show for the rest of his life to ensure he behaved. But she realized she was getting ahead of herself. She needed to focus on this class, this minute, in this ring, not on the future.

Sadie remembered something Captain Vinson said about people changing. Maybe she had changed since the first show. She felt different, and Lucky sure acted differently. Funny, when the Captain said it, Sadie thought about change in a negative way. But today, she embraced change in a positive way.

The ribbons told the story for Sadie and Lucky's first class. Sadie earned her first blue ribbon, and somehow kept herself from screaming. She looked out to see her mom, Austin, and Katie jumping up and down as if she'd won the gold medal at the Olympics. Amanda nodded and smiled. But most precious, Brady pointed to his hat and hollered, "I told you!" reminding her he'd predicted his hat would bring them luck today. Sadie wanted to cry, but instead closed her eyes for a second and silently recited, *this is for you, Dad, and you'll be here next time.*

During the second class, the sky continued to darken and the rain began to fall in big drops leaving splotches in the dirt. No thunder or lightning, so they didn't stop the show. Sadie's wet show clothes soon clung to her, but she worried more about the thick arena sand and puddles Lucky would have to navigate. Sadie's tension rose with the change of weather. With the pressure on after her first blue ribbon, she figured her crowd expected her to win again.

Lucky must have perceived Sadie's nervousness, because the smooth trot he'd had all day got jiggy and short-stepped. That's not what judges looked for in an English pleasure class. Sadie caught herself, controlled her breathing, and tried to relax. But not enough. She listened to the placings, amazed she even got a fourth place. And Rachel came in second.

Now, Sadie needed a repeat performance of her first class in what she considered her most challenging class of the day. In the minutes before her final class, Sadie saw her newfound horse show friend, Fay, sopping wet.

"Hey, Fay, I saw your classes this morning. You looked great."

"Thanks, Sadie. And I even got a ribbon. I had to start the collection at some time, right?"

"Congratulations! I hope it was because you made everything look 'eeeasssyyy,'" Sadie said, wiping raindrops from her face with her gloves and wondering when the rain would stop.

"Your class is about to start, and I'm here to help you make it look easy," she chuckled. "Oh, and I gave your mom a note for you to read later that I hope you'll like. Good luck, now."

Sadie entered the ring to find Rachel and Black Widow standing two steps inside the gate. Sadie tried to avoid her, but caught the dark eyes when she looked up to make sure she didn't run into another horse and rider. The rain took its toll on Rachel's overdone makeup, and the black streaks beneath her eyes made her resemble a zombie.

"I knew you wouldn't get that lucky again," she said, turning her horse with a swift kick and a harsh pull on her bit, prancing off. Even the mare's tail swished.

Sadie thought for a minute, and tried to forget it. But she couldn't. This comment was different. It wasn't about other people; it was about her. The insult didn't make her angry, like the others had. It made her reflective. And in the thirty seconds Sadie had to shake it off before the judging began, she figured it out.

Sadie and Lucky didn't win the first class because of luck. They won because they worked hard. They worked as a team; they learned together; they understood each other, and they forgave each other. Brady may think his hat made them lucky, and she wouldn't dispel his myth. But she knew going into this last class, luck had nothing to do with her wins.

Sadie decided not to worry about Rachel's prediction. Or threat? It didn't matter. Sadie would let the rain wash away her worry. She would continue to work hard, listen to her coach, receive the support of her friends and family, and ride with a purpose.

"Ring one, you are now being judged at a walk. Ring one, all walk, please."

By now, Lucky's purposeful walk showed the judge he was meant to be a show horse. When Sadie had heard of horses with this gene, she didn't realize Lucky would be one of them, particularly after the last show. But while he moved beneath her, she sensed him saying, "Look at me, look at me." These amusing thoughts calmed Sadie, and she enjoyed the ride and her wonderful equine partner. Sadie wasn't going to let her childish nerves ruin this last class.

They trotted in both directions, performing both a sitting trot and a posting trot. Sadie knew Lucky showed best at the trot. Because of his Andalusian breeding, he floated across the ring and made his rider look good. Today, as long as Sadie relaxed, Lucky did, too. And although Sadie couldn't watch the other riders while she showed, the pair would be hard to beat the way he moved right now.

Knowing the canter portion was ready to begin, Sadie snuck a peek at her cheering section and caught Austin's thumbs-up. A few trot steps later, Fay called out, "You're making it look easy," and Sadie smiled both inside and out.

"Ring one, left lead canter, please; ring one, left lead canter."

Time for the big test.

Sadie sat deep, heels down, shoulders back, eased her right leg back a smidge, and asked Lucky to canter. The transition was even smoother than when they practiced, and Sadie hoped the judge was watching. Lucky remained calm, and Sadie continued to squeeze him on, rocking with his three-beat motion. Sadie looked ahead giving herself plenty of time to plan in case she gained on other horses. But at this nice pace, and Lucky paying no attention to the mud, they moved easily and steadily among the pack. Before Sadie knew it, the call came to walk and reverse directions. She wasn't even out of breath.

Jimmy stood right at the rail with Billy and called, "You're almost there," as they passed. Billy nodded in agreement. Sadie knew this was true, but also knew one tiny mistake could determine winning or losing the class. And Sadie didn't want to lose.

"Ring one, right lead canter, please; ring one, all canter."

Lucky got it. Right lead canter right off the bat. Nice and steady and slow, like the last direction. As they reached the long side of the ring past the judge, a rider cut directly in front of them. It was an obvious attempt to fluster Lucky or get him to break his gait. Fortunately, Lucky trusted Sadie enough to know she wouldn't run him into another rider, or a fence. So instead of getting upset, Sadie's horse followed her command to turn the corner early to avoid the black mare with the swishing tail and its dangerous rider.

Once ahead of the problem, Sadie sped Lucky up to create enough distance for them to complete their class in peace. Sadie spoke to Lucky as they cantered away saying, "Good boy, Lucky, good boy. You're the one who makes it look easy."

As they lined up in the center of the ring, Sadie breathed a sigh of relief. Even if they didn't score well, Sadie believed they did their best. She convinced herself winning didn't really matter, when she heard, "We have the results from class 109. In first place, it's Sadie Navarro riding Color Me Lucky; in second place, it's…."

They won.

20

Bullies Don't Rule

At the end of the school day on Wednesday, while waiting for Brady, Sadie remembered Mom finally found Fay's note from the show. Sadie dug in the outside pocket of her backpack and opened the note printed in brown ink on pink paper:

> **To my new friend, Sadie,**
>
> **Since you didn't know what your name meant, I looked it up for you. Turns out, "Sadie" can mean two things: Either "princess," or "mercy." Now, you're not a princess (are you?). But you showed mercy when we first met. So that has to be the meaning of your name. I thought you'd want to know. Good luck to you at the finale, Mercy!**
>
> **Your new friend,**
> **Fay ("Faith")**

What a neat note.

Sadie continued waiting on the bus for Brady, saving the seat next to her like she had done since he moved in next-door in January. No one else ever tried to take the seat, but it was another way Sadie showed Brady she was his loyal friend. Some kids teased others about hanging out with younger kids, but Sadie found this ridiculous. Growing up living on military bases, she learned to try to get along with everyone.

Usually Brady bounded on the bus early, ready to recount his wonders of the day. Sometimes Sadie felt as if she was reliving fourth grade through Brady's eyes, but she didn't stop him. His enthusiasm for school warmed her, and the two friends held different interests. The things Brady found fascinating were often things Sadie hadn't paid much attention to, for instance, history.

Brady relayed the stories of the War of 1812 to Sadie in such finite detail, she nicknamed him "Brady Battles." Brady studied history and told Sadie stories about battles within miles of where they now lived, in a different time. Sometimes Sadie wondered if his focus on the past helped him escape the here and now.

Today Brady boarded the bus last, shoulders slumped, eyes down, as he shuffled into the seat next to his older friend. The driver pulled away, bus gears grinding loud as usual.

"What's wrong?" Sadie asked, wanting to get to the point at once.

"Nothing," he answered, slow and low, clutching his backpack in his lap.

"That's not true," Sadie continued, hoping to coax him into talking.

"I don't want to talk about it," he said, even lower.

"Not even to me?"

"Especially not to you."

"Brady Battles! I don't believe you!" she said, hoping her pet nickname would bring him out of his funk.

"Do you see anything different?" he asked, looking in her eyes. Sadie read the hurt.

"I see you aren't looking too happy."

"My hat! They stole my hat! I tried to stop them, but they tripped me, and they started throwing it to each other, and I couldn't reach it. I'm so sorry, Sadie...." His little shoulders moved with the small sobs he choked back.

"Shhhh, it'll be okay." Sadie saw the bus driver watching in the rearview mirror, and she nodded meaning it was under control. "*You* are sorry? You don't have anything to be sorry about. Now let's stop talking about it because it's obviously upsetting you. We're just going to sit quietly and come up with a plan."

"Okay, a plan. My plan didn't work," Brady pouted, but not crying.

"That's why we're a team. We'll come up with a great team plan, and I guarantee you that you'll be wearing your hat tomorrow." Sadie tousled Brady's hair, convincing herself at the same time they could do it.

They rode in silence for the rest of the bus ride, while Sadie's mind worked hard. Brady stole a glance at her, and Sadie gestured with her second finger, pointing at her chin, imitating the famous statue of "The Thinker." Brady didn't quite smile, but nodded, remembering he was supposed to be devising a plan. Sadie wondered what must be going through poor Brady's mind and wished the driver made those old, noisy gears work faster to get them to their bus stop sooner.

Stepping off the bus, Sadie said, "Let's go," heading to her house. Out in his yard as usual, Grandpa Brogan waved, acknowledging Brady made it home.

"Aaauuussttiinnn!" Sadie yelled, as soon as she entered.

"No, Sadie! You can't tell Austin...please...I mean he gave me—" Brady protested.

"Look, you're working with the Navarro family now, and we work as a team. He's not going to be mad. Well, at least not at you, that is."

Austin appeared at the top of the stairs. "What? Do you have another job or something?"

"Not exactly, but we need your help."

"Okay, I'm on the way."

The three of them sat around the kitchen island, the Navarro siblings allowing Brady to tell his full story. Sadie observed Brady telling his story without crying and realized how brave he was trying to be in front of his hero, Austin, who sat listening, nodding, and thinking. Sadie had seen this look many times.

Austin started, "No reason to dwell on *why*. We all know bullies are bullies because they have their own problems they can't deal with so they take them out on others. So let's focus on how to get your hat back." He sounded so adult.

"I tried, and those Baker twins just made fun of me. And they told me if I told my teacher they would find me later, and...well, you know. They're bigger than me," Brady relayed, sounding shaken, and like he'd been through something similar.

"Austin, I'm sure you are bigger than them. Can you come to our school and tell them to give the hat back? Because you gave Brady the hat?" Sadie asked, proud of herself for coming up with the solution so quickly.

"Good thinking, but I see a few problems. First, what happens when I leave? They may be afraid of me, but this plan continues to leave Brady as a target. Second, getting a bigger kid to intimidate them will perpetuate the problem. Next thing, they'll have someone bigger coming after me. It's an ugly cycle, and not the best approach. But let's keep thinking."

Sadie felt as if her dad had just been in the room. Although she wasn't happy that Austin didn't agree with her idea, Dad's wisdom comforted her here in her brother's skin.

"I could tell my dad," Brady said. "But I did that once, and it caused even more problems. I had to leave the school for good." Sadie and Austin eyed each other and decided not to ask for details.

Sadie broke the silence. "What if I confront them? After all, I'm your friend, and you had the hat because you were my groom?"

"No, I don't want you near those guys. They're mean, and—" Brady's small voice cracked, shaking his head and clenching his teeth.

"Mean? They're kids! They can't be as mean as some of the people I came across while trying to save the horses," Sadie said, taking a stand. "I'm not afraid of a couple of bullies."

Austin sat back, crossing his hands across his chest, tipping back in his chair. "I think we're getting somewhere."

"You want to let your sister take on these guys?" Brady asked, sounding confused.

"Only with a good plan. And that's why we're here. Just like we're doing this as a team, I think we need a team to confront the twins."

"So you *will* come?" Brady asked.

"No, but we already have two on the team — you and Sadie. Now, the Bakers told you not to tell your teacher, but you can't help it if Sadie tells *her* teacher, right?"

"Mr. Edwards! Of course he'll help. Remember his talk about looking out for those who can't look out for themselves, and all. Why didn't I think of that?" Sadie asked.

Brady looked perplexed, then reasoned, "I guess my hat is part of my uniform, working for Sadie, so she has an interest in getting my uniform piece back. And Mr. Edwards, everyone knows who he is, and they'd be crazy to mess with him. I'm in. Let's do it tomorrow."

"Then the plan is settled. Now, Brady, it's time to go," Sadie reminded.

"Go where?"

"We need to go to work with the Desire Horse Club — it's Wednesday. You didn't forget, did you?"

"I can't go, Sadie. Not after today."

"I won't hear that from you. Those kids need you. This isn't about you, it's about them."

"But—"

"No buts, you're going to put a smile on your face and do your job. Besides, I bet you're going to feel better."

"Only for you, Sadie."

"No, for you Brady…and for the kids. Now let's go."

* * *

Sadie and Brady overheard the voices and noise before they turned the corner into the barn. Brady's hands were shoved into his front pants pockets and he wore a visible frown on his face. Sadie motioned with two fingers under her chin, and said, "Chin up." He complied.

"Brady! I'm so glad you are here," Tyler, from last week, called out. "I have to show you something!"

Brady went to where Tyler stood by Hank, the stout chestnut mustang pony standing in the cross ties for grooming. "Look, after you showed me how to do the hooves last week, I've been practicing. I finally got it right! Now watch."

Brady surveyed the small boy leaning against the pony and lifting his hoof. With all his concentration, Tyler picked the hoof clean, and then put it back down on the ground, patting Hank's chubby leg. "Remember, I couldn't do that before?"

"That's great, Tyler. No, I didn't know you couldn't pick hooves. What made the difference?"

"I don't know, a couple of things, I guess. Like first of all, you explained it to me in a way I understood. And you told me that just because the horse was bigger than me, it didn't mean he was in charge."

Sadie took it in from a distance, finding the coincidence interesting.

"You remembered all that from a week ago?" Brady asked.

"Yes, because you made sense to me. I've been trying to pick hooves since last year, when I first started coming here. A few of the other kids teased me because I could never get it right. It wasn't until you helped me. That's when I got it right. I wanted to show you, and let you know. Thanks for the help."

"Oh, it was nothing. Just doing my job. But I'm glad whatever I said worked for you," Brady said, embarrassed by the attention of the other kids in the group.

Sadie's heart warmed as she saw Brady realizing he had something to offer. She could tell he felt better already. Who would have thought that a simple pony and a hoof pick could build confidence in two boys in two different ways?

21

Confrontation

"May I talk to you for a minute after class, please… in private?" Sadie whispered to Mr. Edwards when she passed his desk going toward her seat.

"Sure you can. We need to catch up on your horse therapy project anyway. I've been so busy with the end of the school year coming. Stop by my desk on your way out."

The bell rang, and the class scattered, with the usual increase in volume by twenty decibels.

"So, tell me how your project is going," Mr. Edwards said.

"I hate to tell you this, but this isn't about my project," Sadie said, unhappy to disappoint her teacher. "It's more important."

"More important? You have me curious."

Knowing time was short, Sadie spouted, "Two kids stole my friend's hat, and I need to help him get it back. I promised him I'd get it back today."

"Sadie, we take bullying seriously here at Willis. We're going to need to report this."

"We can, but I need your help first. I wanted to go and confront the Baker twins myself, but Austin suggested I ask for your help. You see, they told my friend—"

"And who is your friend?"

"Brady. Brady Brogan. He's in fourth grade, and the nicest kid."

"Okay, go on, and slow down." Mr. Edwards got up and shut his door, holding up a finger to the kids outside to wait a minute.

"They told Brady they would beat him up if he told his teacher. But the hat is Brady's groom hat that he wears when he helps me at the horse shows. So, it's kind of his uniform. He wore it to school because he was so proud of it. And these jerks preyed on him and took something from him that is so special and means nothing to them."

"I can see you are upset, and I understand. I'm glad you are standing up for your friend, although I'm not surprised. You're a fighter. If I was looking for someone to help me get something back, I'd want you on my side."

"So you'll help?"

"Yes, but give me a little time."

"But I promised…."

"Don't worry, but I need to work this out with the teachers. Unfortunately, I've dealt with these things before. We'll work it out. I'll come get you when it's time."

The day dragged on and on. Sadie watched the big black hand on the white face of the clock click by so slowly she wanted to scream. And Brady. He probably figured Sadie had abandoned him. She felt terrible.

Minutes before lunch, Mr. Edwards got Sadie out of math class. He whispered to her teacher, who pointed to Sadie to go with Mr. Edwards and he looked all business. But he also looked proud, like although he disapproved of the situation, he approved of its current progress.

"Here's how it's going to go. The Baker boys and Brady are in the library, with the librarian, Mrs. Hawkins. She wanted to join the team, too." Mr. Edwards smiled, shifting out of his total-businesslike demeanor for a second. Mr. Edwards knew Sadie liked the librarian, who had helped her in various ways since Sadie arrived at the school.

"Brady's teacher knows what's going on. Anyhow, I will bring you in, and I'll ask Brady what he has to say. He will ask for his hat back, and experience tells us the boys will not give it back to him. This is where you step in."

"And I tell them the hat is part of his uniform, and he needs it. And then I politely ask for it, right?"

"Your exact words are up to you, but yes, after we've given them a chance to resolve it at the lowest level, and they haven't, is when you'll need to step in."

"If they are smart, they will give you the hat, and we'll be done. If not, I take action. And let's hope it doesn't get there, because they don't want to make Mr. Edwards madder than he is. As you probably know, I detest bullies."

"Yes, I figured as much." Sadie smiled, lightening the intense moment.

"Not everyone would do this, Sadie. Brady's lucky to have you as his friend. Now, are you ready?"

"Of course I'm ready," Sadie said, sounding more confident than the reality of her shaky knees.

The three boys sat around a table at the back of the library where Mrs. Hawkins hovered. Brady pretended to read the book in front of him, and the other two boys, looking exactly alike, poked each other and made faces. Sadie hated to judge, but she disliked them at once. They wore bright-colored oversized hockey jerseys and super short military-style haircuts. Sadie didn't need them to stand up to picture their jeans hanging low exposing their boxer shorts. She also surmised that they got great delight from doing disgusting things like putting pencils up their noses.

"Mrs. Hawkins, will you join us, please?" Mr. Edwards began. "Boys, sit up straight, and pay attention," he commanded. The hoodlums looked at him as if he had two heads, but recognized who was in charge and shifted in their seats. Mr. Edwards was bigger, but he didn't need to be. These kids realized he was serious.

"Brady, you have something to say, right?" Mr. Edwards encouraged.

Poor Brady! Sadie thought. He had to be dying inside.

"No, it's nothing, really," Brady said, face ghost white.

"That's not true, Brady. As I understand, these boys took something of yours. Let's give them the opportunity to give it back," Mr. Edwards stated.

"My hat fell off yesterday when I tripped. I asked for it back, but they threw it over my head and kept it. And I think they have it. At least that's what I think happened," Brady said, each word less audible.

You mean when they tripped you! Sadie wanted to shout, but didn't.

"What do you say, boys?" Mr. Edwards asked,

giving them a chance.

"We don't have his stupid hat. Why would we want his hat?" said the one in the Washington Capitals jersey.

"Yeah, I mean, we have our own hats. Why would we want this dweeb's?" the one wearing the Philadelphia Flyers jersey snickered.

"Stop the name calling — now!" a voice boomed that Sadie had never heard from her mentor-teacher. Even Mrs. Hawkins flinched.

Sadie spoke up, "Can I see your hats, please?"

The two looked at Sadie as if she were the rival hockey team. "What's it to you?" The Philadelphia Flyers jersey-wearer challenged her.

"I have an interest. Brady works for me, and that hat is part of his uniform."

"Ha! Sure, boss lady, we can show you our hats," hissed the more boisterous of the two wearing the Washington Capitals shirt. Sadie didn't even want to know their names. Fishing into his backpack, the noisy one pulled out a ball cap matching his jersey, reading "CAPITALS." While Mr. Edwards looked toward the other brother, Washington stuck his tongue out at Sadie, who wished she was elastic woman so she could reach across and pull it out.

With that picture in her mind, Sadie said, "That's one. Where's the other?"

Philadelphia Flyers reached into his backpack and produced a second hat. The hat read "GROOM" across the front. "And here's mine. All mine."

"Looks an awful lot like Brady's hat," Sadie said.

"What? He's the only one who has a hat saying 'GROOM'? They sell these all over."

"You could be right. I didn't realize they were so popular. I thought Brady's was one of a kind."

"You were wrong," said Washington Capitals, in a guttural voice sending chills through Sadie, who looked to Brady and saw him terrified. He looked lost.

Infuriated, but steady, Sadie asked politely, "Can I see your hat, please?"

Philadelphia Flyers tossed the hat at Sadie, trying to shoot it far over her head. She reached up and caught it. "Not bad for a girl, huh?" she asked, feeling empowered now.

She faced the GROOM inscription directly at the brothers, and asked, "So you are sure this is your hat, right?"

They both nodded, relaxed, as if they had all the answers. They looked to each other, as if needing confirmation, and nodded back to Sadie.

"Well then, why does it say BRADY on the back?" She left the question hanging. She showed Brady's inscription, in turn, to Mr. Edwards, Mrs. Hawkins, and the two boys. Sadie figured these two hadn't looked at the hat. They didn't want the hat. They wanted to exert power over a defenseless kid.

But they picked the wrong kid.

"Please don't do something like this again. You don't want this girl to come after you."

Brady was speechless.

"I need to get to lunch now," Sadie said, closing out the event.

"I'll take you," Mrs. Hawkins offered, sounding relieved. "And you, too, Brady. Let's go."

"And you two, you're coming with me. I tried to give you a chance, but you blew it. Bullying, stealing, and lying...we're going to talk to the principal about this one. We can't let this go. And considering your mom is the principal, I can't imagine life is going to be good for you two for a while."

On the way back to class, Brady sheepishly asked Mrs. Hawkins, "Could I talk to Sadie for just a second, please?"

"Sure, Brady. This has been quite an ordeal for you. Go ahead." Mrs. Hawkins gave them space so he could talk in private.

"I don't know what to say. You are the best friend I've ever had. How can I ever repay you?" Brady asked, earnest eyes searching Sadie's face.

"You don't need to repay me. I want you to be happy. Wait a minute, maybe you can. Someday, you help someone else like this, okay? Except I know I wouldn't have to ask that. It's who you are, Brady Battles. You are always a winner in my book."

Brady reached up, and Sadie felt his awkward little hug. She looked at Mrs. Hawkins who knew kids weren't supposed to touch each other in school. Sadie squeezed him, backed up, and asked, "Now where's that hat?"

Brady pointed to her, and Sadie placed it back on his head where it belonged. Tapping the top of his head, she said, "Now keep it there," and the two smiled. A shared victory.

22

Facing Fears

Austin drove Sadie to her final visit to the Caisson Platoon Equine Assisted Programs, closing out her internship. Sadie fidgeted, played with the radio, and could not settle down. She had to talk.

"Austin, we can always be honest with each other, right? Best friends through six moves. Only friends sometimes. If I tell you something, do you promise not to tell anyone?"

"That's always such a dumb question. I mean, if you told me you killed someone, I'd have to tell someone, right? But, since I don't think you killed anyone, go ahead."

"I'm serious!"

"Wow, okay, sorry. I'm all ears."

"Austin, I'm scared to death."

"Of what?"

Where did she begin...of Dad getting killed or

maimed, or being afraid of dealing with people who remind her that Dad may be killed or maimed. Or being afraid of dealing with people she's never dealt with, who are expecting her to help them. She decided on an answer, "Of working with the wounded veterans."

"I guess that's understandable, it's new to you. But you can do anything. You've proven it time and time again. Why should you be afraid?" When he turned to look at Sadie, she felt him look as if he was looking for someone else to be sitting in the seat.

"I can't explain it, but I'm so nervous. I kept thinking it would pass, but we're almost here, and it hasn't gone away yet."

"Okay, remember the story *The Wizard of Oz*? We used to watch it on television every year — it's a really, really old movie. Starts in black and white, changes to color…"

"Yes, sure I do. But what does that have to do with this?"

"Remember the lion, the Cowardly Lion? He doubted himself. He didn't think he had courage. But he had it the whole time, and proved it over and over again. You have courage, too, Sadie. Sometimes you just don't know it."

"Thanks," Sadie said, having hoped for a better answer.

"I'll come with you, if it will make you feel better. But you're not going to need me. You'll find your courage."

They traveled the last few miles in silence, while Sadie tried to concentrate on something other than what was about to happen. She arrived at Fort Belvoir wiping her clammy hands on her pants in case she had to shake someone's hand. She brought Austin with her to meet Captain Vinson, hoping deep inside he would tell her today's activities had been canceled for one reason or another — maybe the heat. Instead, she heard a friendly greeting.

"So who is this here? Another recruit?" Captain Vinson asked, extending his giant hand to reach for Austin's. Sadie saw Austin grip hard as the two exchanged a man-to-man smile.

"Captain, this is my brother, Austin. Remember I talked about him last time? I hope it's not a problem he's here. He won't interfere, I wanted him to come along, for..."

"It's not a problem. He even looks like he's old enough to volunteer."

"Thanks, Sir, I'm seventeen. But this horse stuff is Sadie's gig. I was going to sit in the car and call my girlfriend. But since it's Sadie's last time here, and she's pretty excited about it, I thought I'd come along and support her."

"Well thanks for supporting your sister, son. If you decide to volunteer, get in touch. For now, I'm going to get Sadie tracking for our plans today. There's a bench over there," he pointed toward a wooden bench with a back and a side table beneath the shade trees. "You can hang out and watch from a distance. And you can use your cell phone there if you want."

"Thanks, I'll do that." Austin headed toward the sitting area and turned back over his shoulder to Sadie saying, "Roar, Sadie, roar."

Captain Vinson looked at her as if he hadn't heard right.

"It's a brother-sister thing," she explained through

a smile.

The captain nodded and got back to business.

"So here's the plan. You are going to help me do my job today, helping at the grooming station." He brought her out to the same grooming station as the last time, several large wooden poles anchored in a sand footing. "Help where you're needed, and be yourself. I'll go get our first horse and rider."

Captain Vinson entered the grooming area with a huge black gelding whose head was as long as Sadie's arm. While Captain Vinson secured the horse to the grooming station cross ties, he spoke: "Sadie, this here is Berner, and as you can see, he's a lot to groom."

Before Sadie had time to let her anxiety build, she heard a voice from behind the massive Berner. "I'll say. Good thing I got some real help today, Captain, instead of the usual," the young man joked. He didn't look much older than Austin, but he was much shorter, and wore his hair tightly cropped. A prosthetic device on his right leg didn't seem to slow him down.

"And meet Private Shane Schmidt," Captain Vinson said. "If nothing else, he'll keep you entertained. So, I'll leave you two and be back in a few. Holler if you need me." The captain lumbered off.

Sadie barely noticed the injury she had been fearing, accepting instead the warm, kind, expression the young man offered her.

"So what brings you here?" the private asked. "You look kind of young."

So do you. "I'm sorry, I figured someone told you. I'm here because I want to learn about different kinds of equine-assisted activities. I'm not old enough to volunteer yet, but since I was so interested, they decided to let me come visit a few times to learn."

"Why the Caisson Platoon?" he asked, currying the dirt from the thick black coat, causing dust clouds to rise.

"My teacher found it." She sounded so feeble. "He thought it would be good since my dad is in Afghanistan."

"Well, Semper Fi then, kid."

"That's the Marine Corps motto — 'Always Faithful' — my dad taught me that!" Sadie wanted to let Private Schmidt know she knew something about the military. And she worked hard to keep up with his brisk grooming.

"Dad's a Marine?"

"No, Navy. But he's a big fan of the Marines. He said if he hadn't gone into the Navy, he would have been a Marine."

"Second best isn't too bad, if he had to go into the Navy instead." The private smiled, making eye contact. His mannerisms and informal demeanor put Sadie at ease, as he continued. "So, fire away — what questions do you have for me?"

Sadie allowed the words to rise from her heart, barely audible, "Are you afraid to ride?"

"Me? No, but I used to be. I've found when I focus on what I *can* do instead of what I *can't* do, it's a whole lot better. Why, are you afraid to ride?"

Sadie thought he was making fun of her, but she realized he asked an honest question. He only knew her as the kid here asking him stupid questions. "Of course not!" she answered, with confidence. "I have my own horse, and his name is Lucky. We're competing for the first time this summer."

"Tell me more. I want to compete someday. I want to do Western. Seems more fun than bumping up and down on a tiny saddle in dressy clothes," he said. He imitated a person posting up and down, lips pursed and making his face and neck long, looking snooty.

Sadie laughed. "Wait a minute — that's what I do! And it's not as easy as it looks."

"What can be so hard about this?" He mock posted again, this time turning his head side to side and nodding, as if greeting fans.

Sadie started speaking faster, like she did when getting excited. "For instance, at my first show with Lucky, he wasn't used to the crowds, and he missed his horse buddy. He was a nervous wreck! He whinnied, and cried, and wouldn't listen at all. It was so hard to keep him under control, and I didn't look anything like what you just looked like!"

"And you weren't afraid?" he asked, peeking under Berner's neck at her.

Sadie stopped. "I guess I was. But I hadn't really thought about it that way."

"I'll forgive you for lying to me then. By the way, you're doing a great job of helping. Berner doesn't stand this good most of the time, but he's learning."

Sadie blushed. "Thanks. Now, back to the show, so, it's not always so easy. But you can only do the best you can do. Right?"

"You're awfully smart for a kid."

"Not really. Not about some things," Sadie said, staring at the brush she used on Berner.

"What's that supposed to mean?"

"I have dumb ideas about things sometimes," she answered, thinking about her apprehension of being around people like this friendly, funny private.

"That's normal. Sometimes people are surprised

by my positive outlook on life. But hey, I'm alive. And that's more than many can say." He stopped brushing and looked Sadie in the eye again, serious this time. "Sometimes you gotta go on — not only for you, but for them." After a few seconds, he went back to his precise grooming, and patted Berner.

"I'll remember that," Sadie finally answered. He had no idea what her dumb ideas were, but he shared his valuable advice without hesitation.

"Okay, Private, let's get moving," Captain Vinson suggested. "I'll bring Berner over to the ring, and Sergeant Major will meet us at the mounting block. Time to say goodbye, Sadie. I'll be back in a minute with your next pair."

"So, you coming back next week, kid?"

"I'm afraid not. This was my final internship session. It's been an awesome experience, and I've learned so much. But hopefully I'll be back when I'm old enough to be a real volunteer in a few years."

"I hope so. People can use your help. But, I have to admit, I hope I'll be gone. I hope to either be back in the field in the Marine Corps or back home in Pennsylvania. I'm sure they miss me in both places," he smiled.

"Good luck with your Western riding. I've done that, too, and you'll be great!" Sadie called, as the private departed for the mounting block. She needed to dedicate a ride in her new Western saddle in honor of this brave hero the next time she rode. Semper Fi, Private Shane Schmidt.

Moments later, Captain Vinson returned with a new horse for the grooming station, and a young woman, dark hair pulled back in a braid. Strangely, Sadie thought, this woman could be an older version of herself.

"Sergeant Marie Silva, this is Sadie Navarro, the

one I told you about," Captain Vinson said. Sadie wondered what he had told her. Sergeant Silva did not have full use of the left side of her body. Or, correction, from what Sadie learned today, Sergeant Silva *could* use the right side of her body, and had *some* use of the left side of her body.

"It's nice to meet you, Sadie. If you are ready to get to work, you can help me clean up Ben." Sadie liked her get-to-work attitude right away.

Sergeant Silva grabbed the currycomb out of the tack box and began working the large gray draft gelding on his left side. The gray arched his neck away from her in an invitation to rub there more. "I love this guy. Ben thinks he's a big dog. He's one of my favorites."

"So, you've been coming here for a while?"

"Yes, it's been very helpful. I've gained a lot of strength and balance. And these guys," she patted Ben with her stiffer left hand, "have a way of connecting with the soul like no other animals."

"I know. I love horses," Sadie offered, while brushing the dirt off of the huge gray legs with a hard grooming brush.

"So what have you done with your life so far, other than love horses?"

Sadie wasn't sure how to respond. Sergeant Silva didn't want to hear her life story. It had to be boring compared to her own. And at the rate she was grooming, she didn't even have time to talk about the past year. Hearing the silence, Sadie filled it. "I saved ten horses from an auction and found them new homes." It sounded so stupid. These people put their lives on the line. And the best Sadie could come up with was she saved some animals.

"That's amazing — wow — when I was your age I

couldn't have done that. So now are you here to save us?" The female soldier pointed to herself with her free hand.

"No, not at all! I'm just here to help." Sadie was mortified the sergeant thought Sadie believed she could do that. "I want to help with horse therapy. I've learned the best way to understand things is to get in there and do them. Like with the ten horses." Sadie needed to stop blabbing about the horses.

"I was kidding. We don't see many kids here, so you must be pretty special for Sergeant Major and Mary Jo to let you help."

"Sergeant Major?"

"Yes, Sergeant Major Pence, the cofounder. That's what most of us call him. He's a retired Army sergeant major. We have a lot of respect for that."

"I understand that, too. I have a lot of respect for everyone around here. Oh, and to answer your question, no I'm not special, I'm just fortunate. It's been great meeting you, and I hope I can help in some way today."

"You already have, Sadie, by taking the time to talk. You'd be surprised at how some people just stare, afraid to talk for some reason."

"Oh, I'm not afraid to talk. Ask anyone. Sometimes people think I talk too much."

"Can I answer any questions about the horses and what happens here for you?"

"Well, yes, if you don't mind. You see, I've had a chance to learn about therapeutic riding at one place, and how it helps children with autism. And I'm volunteering at another place, where I'm learning how horses help kids learn responsibility. And am I already talking too much?"

"No, please go on. I enjoy your enthusiasm." Sergeant Silva now maneuvered Ben's first hoof into position to pick it out. She caught Sadie watching, and said, "Go on; I'm fine. I'm interested in your question."

"Since you're only the second person I've talked to who is an actual client of this program, would you mind telling me your opinion of what's best about it?"

"Excellent question, and an easy answer. But now you'll have to tell me if I'm talking too much. It's an easy answer, but not a short one." She took a breath, and moved on to Ben's next hoof.

"I had a successful Army career and everything going for me. When I got injured in Iraq, everything changed. I went through a rough time where I felt depressed and worthless, and even suicidal. I lost hope."

Sadie filled the quiet space again, now regretting she had asked the stupid question. "Can I help with last two hooves?"

"If you must. But it's not because I need the help."

"I understand. But you are working and talking, and I'm just standing here when I'm supposed to be helping."

"Fair enough. So, where was I, oh, I met Mary Jo out at the Walter Reed Medical Center, and she invited me to take part in the program. She sensed I needed help. While I've made great strides physically, it has been the emotional healing that's been strongest. I see my Army brethren here; I'm on a base; I'm still part of the team. Even the horses are in the military! We cheer each other on and celebrate our successes. It's the camaraderie and the fact of knowing that so many people care about what happens to us. That's what separates this program from the rest.

"After hitting bottom, this place gave me confidence. Now I know nothing can stop me, not even a bomb.

I may do things a different way, but if I set my mind to something, I can do it. Does that answer your question?"

Sadie hesitated to answer, soaking it in. Now she was glad she had asked the question. "Sure does, Sergeant, and thank you for everything — your answer, your service, and your honesty. I really appreciate it. I could never learn all this from a book."

"Just in time, here's the captain. Don't you love him? He's like Ben, one of my favorites. He tries to be all tough on the outside, but on the inside he's a marshmallow."

"I recognize your look there, Sergeant. You'd better not be telling our future volunteer stories about me. She may not come back."

"Oh, she'll be back. Trust me. If she sets her mind to something, she will do it." The sergeant winked at Sadie.

"No doubt," he answered. "Sadie, why don't you come on over with us? Our job here at the grooming station is done for the day, but you can observe Sergeant Silva's riding session if you'd like to. She already agreed."

"Thank you. I'd love to, and I won't even offer to help." The two girls exchanged a knowing grin.

Captain Vinson introduced Sadie to Sergeant Major Pence, the cofounder of the program. He thanked Sadie for her work and said he hoped she'd gotten what she needed while there. Sadie wanted to answer, "You have no idea...." and go on and on. But she could tell the Sergeant Major needed to get to work. She thanked him for letting her take part, told him she had everything she needed to finish her project, and said she'd be back in a few years.

Sadie stood at the fence with Captain Vinson watching the horse and rider team. The Army soldier side-walker in his uniform black cowboy shirt and jeans moved alongside without interfering. Sergeant Silva directed Ben where she wanted him to go. She used a combination of her hips and the single-handed rein holder Mrs. Beckman showed Sadie on day one, so long ago. After the sergeant weaved in and out of a series of lined up poles, she brought Ben to a perfect square halt. Everyone cheered, and Sadie cheered the loudest, uninhibited.

Sadie had never met such brave people. They didn't want anyone to feel sorry for them, and they didn't want anyone to do things for them. She comprehended the theme: they weren't disabled, just differently-abled. Their strength empowered Sadie and enlightened her about change and future possibilities. She wanted to move from the past into the present and to let go of worries doing nothing but polluting her mind. These brave souls she'd been so fearful of led her from the darkness to a new light.

At the end of the session, Captain Vinson offered to walk Sadie and Austin to their car. Austin had been a trouper, and true to his word, stayed out of the way. Sadie wondered why she felt she needed him as a crutch a few hours ago. She hadn't given him a thought since he took his seat under the trees.

Always-intuitive Austin said, "I'll let you two say your goodbyes, and I'll go start the car. It's going to be hot in there. It was nice to meet you, Sir," he nodded, in respect.

Sadie waited a moment, and found her courage. "Captain, before I go, I have a confession to make. I was scared to death to work with the veterans. With my dad still gone, and with everything else…I don't know. I'm sorry, it scared me."

"I know, Sadie; it's why I wanted you to do it.

Thank you for facing your fears. I hope you feel better now."

The gruff old teddy bear gave her a warm hug and patted her on the back. The people Sadie had feared most taught her lessons of a lifetime.

23

Training Day

Rachel screeched to a halt on the gravel in a tiny old red two-seater convertible in front of Loftmar's outdoor arena.

"Who is that?" Erin asked, looking up from her saddle as she and Jimmy cleaned tack on the bench outside the barn.

"A girl from school," Jimmy mumbled, looking at Billy's bridle in his hands. "She's here to ride with me."

Erin looked at Rachel, then Jimmy, and said, "Have fun." She gathered her tack and left. Fast.

"Thanks," Jimmy said, beginning to sweat.

"Well, knock, knock...anyone home?" Rachel asked, flipping her hair, helmet cocked under her arm.

"Who's there? Wait a minute, that's not the way it works," Jimmy said, with a faint laugh. "I see you found it okay — ready to ride?"

"Sure am. You said we can get to a trail here, right?

Trails are great for training horses, if you can ride. You do trails, don't you?"

"Of course I do. And Sadie said it was okay to take Lucky on the trail? I mean, she goes on the trail with him, but—"

"Geez, I already told you she said I could ride him. I told her I'd help fix her horse, and she agreed. I really shouldn't be doing the favor since they did better at the second show. But I'll still win. Besides, at least you and I get a chance to ride together," she said, stepping closer.

Looking toward Sadie's house, Jimmy said, "I just wonder why Sadie didn't mention any of this."

"Oh, silly, don't you see she's embarrassed? She looks up to you, an older, good-looking boy. She doesn't want to admit she still needs help with her horse from someone who has more experience and can ride better than she can."

"It just seems weird that she didn't want to be here."

"She's young, Jimmy, and I don't think she wanted to interfere with our date," she teased, making a smooching sound.

"Our *date*?' I wouldn't exactly call this—"

"Oh hush, let's get ready."

Jimmy helped Rachel groom Lucky, correcting her sloppy work. He pulled out Sadie's new Western saddle, a birthday gift from her grandmother.

"You know, Rachel, you haven't been very nice to Sadie. She's an odd kid to share her horse with you."

"Please — don't you remember how awful this horse was at the first show? Crying and crying until his stupid horse friend showed up?" she said, making whiney whinny sounds.

"Watch it, the stupid horse friend is my Billy," he defended.

"Oh, you know what I mean. He was awful. My Widow would never do something like that because I've trained her right."

"You know Lucky just turned five, right? And he's never horse showed. You know how young horses are."

Rachel waved her hand in the air. "No excuse. Anyhow, I can't see how you don't understand that I am the one doing *her* a favor."

"Well, that Sadie is one-of-a-kind. But we're ready now. Let's go ahead and use the mounting block in the outdoor arena," Jimmy suggested.

"Mounting blocks are for sissies. You can't hop up there on your own, cowboy?"

"Well, of course I can, but it's supposed to be better on the horse's back with the mounting block. But I guess this time, I can do it your way." He smiled, sweating again. "Like in the Wild West or something."

"Good, now we're talking."

Rachel mounted Lucky, swinging her leg hard over his back, yanking the reins and pulling the bit to the back of his mouth. Lucky startled, and lurched back.

"Take *that*, you stupid baby," Rachel yelled, smacking Lucky with the extra length of the Western reins with a loud crack.

"Hey, take it easy, cowgirl. He's not used to that."

"Of course he's not, and it's why he gets away with whatever he wants. I told the girl I'd help fix her horse, and it won't be by babying him. She's obviously done enough of that."

"Easy, Lucky, it's okay," Jimmy reassured.

Jimmy hopped on without incident, and the two

walked single file past the pony fields, headed for the trail.

"Here, take a few pictures with my phone," Rachel ordered. She pulled Lucky to a halt and tossed her phone to Jimmy, spooking Billy in the process. "Sorry. Good pictures now," she demanded. "My Facebook friends will love this."

"Okay, you ready? One, two, and...."

"No, not yet. Hold on. Here we go." Rachel dug her heels hard into Lucky's sides and jerked back on his face with force. Completely confused, Lucky started to back up when she repeated the confusing commands. "Hi ho, Silver, away!" she hollered, now pulling up on his reins with one hand, and slapping his hindquarters loudly with the other.

Jimmy looked through the phone's camera, not sure what he was seeing, but knowing it wasn't good.

"C'mon, you stupid idiot, rear!"

"Rear?!!" Jimmy said, horrified. "Don't do that; rearing is the most dangerous thing you can do on a horse. He has no idea what you are asking him to do."

"Oh, stop being such a worrywart, it's just for the picture."

"No, Rachel, I think you'd better stop. Sadie wouldn't like this."

"Well, if Sadie controlled her own horse, I wouldn't have to be here now, would I? Now come *on*, Lucky, *up*!"

Lucky showed that he had taken all he could. Not being able to move forward due to the tight pull of the reins, he moved back to try to get away from the hurt in his mouth. With banging heels in his sides, and noise and commotion on top of him, he backed straight into a tree. A large, sharp branch broke off with an excruciating crack. Trying to get away from yet another terrifying sound, Lucky bolted, but the branch remained attached to the back of his saddle. The noise on his back turned into a shriek. Rachel slipped off the right side, falling out of the stirrup into a pile at the base of the tree.

Lucky's girth came loose, and his saddle now turned completely underneath his belly. Instinctively, he kicked at the foreign object beneath him which he likely saw as a monster. Still in shock from all that happened, Lucky kicked, kicked, and kicked, tossed his head, and spun around in circles. Finally, the saddle shook free and fell to the ground with a thud. Exhausted, Lucky looked around, dropped his head, and let out a deep sigh.

Jimmy had hopped off of Billy, and he remained calm through this disaster. Jimmy grabbed Lucky and pulled him clear of the saddle and the lump. "Rachel, are you okay?"

Rachel remained in a ball by the tree, on her knees with her arms and hands over her head. "Is it safe now?"

"Yes, I have Lucky. And I think he's fine."

"Good thing he didn't kill me." She winced as she stood up. "Now let me at him. That horse needs a beating."

"No, Rachel, I can't let you do that. We need to go back now."

"Fine then," she seethed. "I don't want to fix him anymore anyway. Our date is over."

24

Redemption

After Jimmy led both horses back to the barn, he said, "We need to call Sadie."

"Why do we need to do that? He seems perfectly fine. I'll just tell Sadie at the next show that I stopped by to ride, and it didn't work out." Rachel paced. "I don't think you need to worry her with all this."

"Lucky is limping. He's lame. He's *not* perfectly fine."

Jimmy pulled his phone out of his side pocket and hit the call button. Rachel stared through three rings.

"Hello?" Sadie answered.

"Hey, Sadie, it's Jimmy, at the barn."

"What's going on?"

"I'll tell you when you get here. You're close by, right?"

"I'll be there in two minutes. Everything's okay, isn't it?" she asked, panicked.

"Yeah, everything's fine. But you need to check out Lucky. See you in a minute." He hung up, staring at Rachel. "You don't look so good; why don't you sit down."

"You don't need me here. I think I'll just leave now. Ta ta."

"Oh no you don't." Jimmy stood in front of her. "No way are you leaving me here to carry the bag on this one."

"No worries," Rachel said, departing the barn. "I won't be far."

As Jimmy opened Lucky's stall door to get a closer look at his possible injury, the tiny loud red car peeled out, spewing gravel.

* * *

Sadie ran down the hill toward Loftmar because she detected something in Jimmy's voice other than "fine." Something was wrong. She felt it and sensed it. A car sped by on the driveway, unusual since most people drove the 10 miles-per-hour posted speed limit. Sadie barely caught a glimpse of the driver as she flew past, but recognized something familiar. And wearing a helmet? How strange.

Sadie arrived at the bottom of the hill out of breath. With Lucky in his stall, at least he wasn't missing. Lucky whinnied like he often did when she arrived, but she detected pain in his voice. Jimmy stood by Lucky's stall, looking down, and not looking at all like the normal Jimmy.

"What's wrong?"

Jimmy lifted his eyes, and Sadie noted the same pain in his eyes she caught in Lucky's whinny. "I'm an idiot," the forlorn voice spoke.

"What are you talking about?"

Jimmy relayed the story to Sadie, who couldn't believe the words as she listened.

"So you did *what*?"

"I can repeat the story later, Sadie, but right now, you need to call the vet."

"Let's find out what Amanda says first." Sometimes it took hours for a veterinarian to arrive, and Sadie needed to understand right away how serious this might be. With any luck, Lucky may have been sore initially, but the sting of having kicked something might wear off in time. Horse injuries could be like that; they could look awful and not mean much. Or, they could not look like much, and be awful. Sadie hoped and prayed for a minor injury.

While still in his stall, Sadie patted Lucky, touching him lightly on parts of his body to gauge his reaction. She picked up his front left hoof, and bent his leg at the fetlock. All was well. She moved to his left hind leg, and he wouldn't budge. Sadie clucked at him, encouraging him to pick up his foot, but he refused. She looked up to find Jimmy returning with Amanda, who looked concerned, but tried to appear upbeat.

"Let's see what we have here. Jimmy said Lucky had some kind of accident?"

Sadie fumed. *Accident?! If you call having some moron perform circus tricks on my horse an accident, well then I guess so.* "I can give you the full details later. But the important part is that he backed into a tree, kicked at his saddle, got stuck on a branch, and who knows what else…all while I wasn't here." Sadie glared at Jimmy. She couldn't believe she once thought he was cute.

Amanda asked Sadie to walk Lucky up the barn aisle, watching carefully. No question, he was lame. The stable manager prodded and pulled his limbs, and Lucky allowed her, recognizing the hands of an experienced horse person. Even though he flinched, he seemed to know the investigation served a purpose. Amanda's eyebrows raised, her lips pursed, and she reported her findings.

"Yep, I'll call Dr. Reese. Lucky doesn't have any open wounds, but something's going on. We need a vet to diagnose it. I have to go re-dish feed now, but come tell me exactly what happened in a few minutes, Sadie. We like to know these things for the safety of the barn."

"I'll come tell you," a muted, shaky male voice said. "It's all my fault, so let me explain so something like this never happens again. Sadie and Lucky had nothing to do with me being so stupid."

And for the first time, Sadie felt slightly sorry for the miserable-looking Jimmy.

After Amanda left, Jimmy said, while walking away, "I'll go get your saddle."

"My saddle?" Sadie couldn't contain her voice. "You let her use my saddle?"

"Yes, Sadie. I'm sorry. I didn't know."

"Why on earth would you think it was okay to let that horrible girl ride my horse and use my saddle? Are you crazy?"

"I'm sorry, Sadie. But I believed her because you are always so nice to everyone. It didn't make a lot of sense to me, but then again you're not the typical thirteen-year-old girl. I asked her, and she said you said she could ride Lucky sometime. I didn't think she would lie to me. I kind of thought she liked me."

Sadie resurrected the blur of the first show and remembered an encounter in the ring. She remembered wanting to get far away from Rachel and not thinking hard about what she was saying to her. *Did this girl really use Lucky to get close to Jimmy? How desperate was that?*

"Help. I can't read your mind." Now that sounded like the old Jimmy. And as angry and worried as Sadie was, she realized Jimmy actually thought Sadie had approved of this girl riding her horse...with him. Things like this made her question whether she would ever understand men.

"Let's go get my saddle. And for the record, if I want someone to ride Lucky, I'll tell you, personally. Okay?"

"Okay. I can't tell you how sorry I am. I'll stay with you until the vet arrives."

Jimmy and Sadie retrieved her Western saddle. Sadie tried not to cringe when surveying the damage. She hoped the saddle took more damage than Lucky did.

25

Down for the Count

Dr. Reese performed a series of tests watching Lucky walk and trot and palpating his legs. She tilted her head right and left, examined his legs up and down again, and asked Sadie to jog him again. Sadie led him at a trot while the veterinarian observed.

Lucky's "girlfriend," Nessa, poked her head out over her stall door each time he passed. It seemed she understood his pain and wanted to help. She let out a shrill whinny on Sadie's third trip jogging the barn aisle as if saying "stop!" Sadie marveled at horse communication and felt touched by the mare's caring.

Dr. Reese said, "Okay, that's enough."

Lucky had splints, an injury caused by many things, but in this case, most likely from kicking out and striking a tree at full force. The good news: he would recover. The bad news: the typical recovery period lasted sixty days.

Lucky would miss the last show of the season, the grand finale, which Sadie had trained for all year. The demonstration to her dad of all they accomplished while he was gone. Sadie's goal: denied.

Sadie could not look at Jimmy.

Dr. Reese provided the equivalent of horse ibuprofin, phenybutazone or "bute," for Lucky's pain for a few days, and a cream to rub on his injury to reduce swelling. Lucky would still be able to go out into the field with his horse friends, but he couldn't be ridden for two months. And while Lucky would recover from his injury, he would need to be reconditioned after his time off. Sadie listened, still stunned. She tried to see the bright side. But she failed to come up with something bright.

Amanda bid Dr. Reese farewell, and Jimmy decided it was time for him to go. He shook his head and said, "I wish I could take it back. I'm sorry. I feel terrible."

From somewhere deep inside her, a voice Sadie didn't recognize croaked, "It's okay. I know you didn't do this on purpose. It's not your fault."

After Jimmy dragged himself out of the barn, Amanda turned to Sadie. "I know it's been a heck of a day, but do you want to talk?"

"There's not much to talk about. Lucky is hurt. We can't show. My dad won't see me. And my new saddle that my favorite grandma gave me for my birthday is broken to smithereens. I can't figure out why I'm not hysterical."

"You're not hysterical because you're a survivor, that's why. But I have an idea. Want to hear it?"

"Sure," Sadie answered, mentally whipped.

"Do you want to compete on one of the Loftmar horses in the grand finale?"

"What?"

"The way this show circuit works, both the horse and the rider accumulate points for the year. You've done well, Sadie, as a rider. And you can still accumulate points in the last show on a different horse."

"But it won't be the same. My final show for Dad was supposed to be the best, and now it's ruined." Sadie now fought to hold back tears.

"You can still do it for your dad, and don't forget, for Lucky. You've been training hard all year," Coach Amanda reminded her. "We have great show horses like Mac, Mic, or Rocky. These guys have done this so many times, they know precisely what to do. One of them will make you look great, Sadie."

"It's not the same."

"You are right. But it's an option, and a good option. Don't let go of your goals now. Besides, you can't let that annoying Rachel beat you. You two are neck in neck. If you give up, she wins. You can't let that happen — Lucky wouldn't want that. And I haven't met your dad yet, but my guess is he wouldn't want you to give up."

"Thanks, Coach. Let me think about it, okay? I appreciate that you care and came up with a plan so fast. But I'm a bit overwhelmed right now."

"I understand. You are welcome, but you don't need to thank me. Remember, we're in this together. I'm here to help. My advice — your best bet would be to show Mac. He's a superstar, and I can see you collecting your grand champion ribbon on him. Let me know in the next few days because we'll have some work to do."

Sadie nodded and left to trudge back up the hill. She heard her dad's voice reminding her in one of his famous quotes: "Never give in." She knew she had her answer.

26

Never Giving In

Saturday morning, Sadie rode Thor in her lesson and remembered again what a joy he was to ride. Sadie's mom told her that animals know who rescued them, and those animals treat their rescuers differently. Sadie experienced this with a dog her family rescued from the pound, but Thor had been her first horse with whom to test this theory. Even though Sadie didn't own Thor, he treated her like a faithful companion. He greeted her at the fence when she walked by outside, stuck his head out the stall door when she passed him in the barn, and obeyed her commands when she rode him.

In the middle of Sadie's lesson, Amanda said, "I have to admit that I thought you were crazy when you said you wanted to take Thor to the grand finale. I'm still not sure what he's going to do when we get there since we've never taken him to a show. But you're doing well with him. Maybe it's your relationship with him."

"Yep, I saved him, and now it's his turn to save me," Sadie said through a smile.

"Let's hope so. I still think you'd be better off with Mac. But this is your decision. Unless you change your mind...."

"No, I'm not changing my mind. Sorry."

"Okay, then. Has anyone ever called you stubborn?" Amanda asked.

Sadie hesitated and looked between Thor's ears, as if she'd find the answer there. "Come to think of it, yes. But I didn't consider it a bad thing."

"Oh, it's not. You'll be fine. Let's get back to work. Your dad's going to be home before you know it," her coach said, defeated in her attempt to persuade Sadie she'd be better off taking one of the proven show horses rather than the unknown entity Thor.

Sadie quickly adjusted to Thor. From somewhere in his background, this seasoned horse understood his job in the ring. Lucky, being young and "green," required far more direction. Thor tolerated Sadie riding him the same way she rode Lucky at first. But Coach Amanda coaxed Sadie into letting Thor convince her that he knew what to do. How nice for Sadie not to have to correct her horse to go straight, turn corners, or maintain the right pace. Thor didn't have Lucky's flashy colors or majestic appearance, but he sure knew his job in the arena.

At 17-hands high, and a thick build due to his draft horse cross breeding, Thor's size drew attention. Although considered a gray horse, most non-horse people called him white. Sadie brushed him twice a day now, even when she didn't ride, to bring out the luster in his coat. He may not be one of the fancy show horses, but Sadie worked to make sure he would look his very best.

Hosing Thor off after their ride to cool and clean him, Sadie felt sad for this kind, hard-working soul. She remembered how he ended up at the auction: a girl owned and showed him and then left for college. Once there, she lost interest, and her parents didn't know what to do with him. So, they sent him to auction. Sadie liked to imagine the parents didn't realize the bad things that can happen to auction horses, or they wouldn't have sent him there. But she would never know.

Sadie wondered how someone could just toss away an animal. Was there more to the story? And what about the scars on his front legs? Sadie found in her experience with horse rescues, the stories weren't always accurate. Sadie couldn't take away Thor's sad past, but she could focus on him here and now. Since coming to Loftmar, people lined up to love this horse. And Sadie was sure he was happier now than when he stood in a pasture by himself, waiting for a girl who never came back to him.

Sadie hugged Thor's wet neck, and he nuzzled her back. She let go, and he took a few steps back, then shook the water off like a dog. Sadie laughed, and covered her mouth, looking around to see where Lucky was. It was silly, but still, she didn't want Lucky to see her playing with Thor, perceiving he'd been replaced. Sadie understood there was only one Lucky, but Lucky may not understand that. She spotted her big pinto at the far end of the geldings' field reaching far across the fence to eat leaves off the bushes. She considered this a good time to let Thor out in the same pasture.

Sadie quietly opened the gate and led Thor in, unhooking the lead rope from his halter. She waited for him to gallop across the pasture to the other horses, but he didn't. He stood there, staring at Sadie. She closed the gate behind her, and stood on the other side. "Go on, now, shoo, go play with your buddies," she said, in horse speak.

Thor rested his head on the gate, looking for one more pet. Sadie reached and stroked his nose, watching his giant brown eyes melt under long thick gray eyelashes. He closed his eyes in what seemed a thank you, and Sadie checked on Lucky's whereabouts again. Good, still fixated on the leaves on the other side of the fence. "Go on, Thor, I have to go. But I'll be back tomorrow, and the next day, and the next. And before you know it, we'll be going to the show!" Thor opened his eyes, let out a deep horse sigh, and turned and plodded off toward his equine companions.

Heading home, Sadie felt bad she'd been complaining all week about attending an event today. She hated the limelight, and today she'd be smack in the middle of it. A month ago, the director of development at Days End Farm Horse Rescue in Woodbine, Maryland, contacted Sadie's mom. Days End invited Sadie to be a featured guest at a large Responsible Horse Ownership event at the farm.

While honored that the largest equine rescue in Maryland invited her to their event, Sadie hated the idea of being on stage. Now she felt selfish for thinking about herself, when she should have been thinking of Thor and all the rescue horses out there. And, now, one of those remarkable rescue horses was going to save Sadie and allow her to achieve her once-lost goal.

27

Days End Farm Horse Rescue

In the car, Sadie's mom seemed almost giddy about today's event. "You should have heard the Days End lady. She said, 'We want to meet this famous horse saver!' I understand you hate the spotlight, but you owe it to the horses." Mom glanced at Sadie in the passenger seat.

"You're right, Mom. Thor straightened me out today. This isn't about me."

Sadie's mom made Austin go, too, since he had been an active player on the "famous horse saver" team. Which of course meant Katie went, too. The hour-long ride up north went by fast, and they began seeing signs for the rescue and for the event. Sadie saw a huge banner at a roundabout that read: "Days End Farm Horse Rescue's Responsible Horse Ownership Day, featuring Maryland Senator Ed Reilly, Award-Winning Band Gaelic Storm, and Famous Horse Saver Sadie Navarro!" She wondered if she could actually die from embarrassment, and if so, how close she was to death at this moment.

"Look, Sadie!" Katie squealed. "Did you know about that?"

Sadie's face burned red. "No." Glaring at her mom, she asked, "Any more surprises, Mom?"

"What? I had nothing to do with this. Why would you think I would do that? Don't you think I know you? Well, hopefully that will be the last surprise of the day," her mom said, sounding like she was apologizing for something she didn't do. Sadie wished she could take back the look. She didn't understand why she blamed her mom when things went wrong. Sadie could tell by Mom's demeanor she had no idea Sadie's name would be plastered along the highways in Northern Maryland, putting her in the same category as a senator and a world-known band.

They arrived after seeing twelve more signs, pulling into a large farm with hilly fence-lined pastures dotted today with large white tents. Music played in the background, and the smell of burgers, hot dogs, fries, and cinnamon buns wafted into the open car windows. Volunteers directed Mom to park among the rows, and rows, and rows of cars.

Austin finally spoke. "Big event."

Sadie sighed. Mom reached over, took her hand, and said, "You'll be fine, sweetheart. You always are."

Sadie nodded, pictured Thor at the fence again, and said, "Thanks. I know."

Tables lined the entrance, and Katie headed to the one with the "V.I.P" sign, saying, "I'll bet you're here."

The woman at the table asked Katie, "Can I help you?"

"Yes, thank you. Is this where Sadie Navarro should check in?"

"Miss Navarro! Such a pleasure to meet you. We're very excited you're here. You are such a role model for our young kids today—"

"Oh, not me," Katie stopped her. "This is Sadie Navarro," she continued, reaching back and pulling Sadie up closer. "I'm just a friend."

Sadie thought for a second, wouldn't that have been nice if Katie could have pretended to be Sadie for today? Instead, she said, "Hi, I'm Sadie. And this is my mom, and my brother, Austin, and you've already met Austin's girlfriend, Katie."

"So nice to meet you all. My name is June Gravitte, and I'm a volunteer here at Days End. I've been particularly interested in meeting you, Sadie, since we live in the same county."

"It's nice to meet you, too Ms. Gravitte. I was told to ask for Ms. Robertson when we arrived."

"Absolutely, if you'll sit tight for a minute, I'll go get her for you."

"Thank you. We appreciate it," Mom answered for the group.

Sadie calculated at least 200 people here, and the all-day event started minutes ago. Thank goodness she didn't have to give a speech. That would put her over the top. The festival atmosphere made it look fun, and from where Sadie stood she viewed pony rides, face painting, an outdoor stage, horse demonstrations, games, and information kiosks. A glorious sunny summer day, a slight breeze kept the heat at bay.

An attractive young brunette wearing a Days End Horse Farm Horse Rescue shirt approached the group with Ms. Gravitte.

"Hello, Mrs. Navarro, I'm Caroline Robertson," she said, extending her hand to Mom. "It's so nice to meet you in person. And you must be Sadie! The famous Sadie!"

Ugh. Sadie hoped this wasn't the theme of the day.

"Hi, and this is my brother, Austin. He helped rescue the horses, too."

"That's wonderful, Sadie — pretty unusual — a brother and sister getting along," she laughed. "We have a big day in store for you here today. Can't you just feel the excitement in the air?"

"I sort of can," Sadie answered, looking at the others for agreement. Heads nodded.

"Let's start with a brief tour for you and your family. After that, you all can wander around as you'd like. But I'll need you at the outdoor stage at 3 o'clock. We'll be doing a presentation for Responsible Horse Ownership Day, followed by a small ceremony hosted by Senator Ed Reilly, who you will adore. And last we'll do our closing events. I hope you like surprises!" she said, her eyes sparkling. She seemed pretty excited about this day, and all Sadie could think was she hoped surprise didn't equal a speech.

Sadie's face must have given away her thoughts. "Oh don't worry, we won't make you say anything if you don't want to. But you might want to...." Ms. Robertson said, looking at each member of their party.

Austin reported, "She won't want to. She doesn't like being the center of attention."

"I can understand that. I don't either, but sometimes it can't be helped. So, everyone, ready for the tour?"

"Ready," Katie spoke for the group.

Ms. Robertson showed them barns, separate holding areas, fields, grooming stations, tack rooms and more. She introduced them to many of the farm's equine residents, relaying stories of how they arrived at Days End. Ms. Robertson spoke at length on the virtues of the many volunteers, without whom the organization would not survive. The group met volunteers who spoke about the horses they worked with fondly and in detail. Sadie realized this was a massive operation and felt even more embarrassed that they made a huge deal over her and her minuscule efforts.

Sadie couldn't decide which she liked best. Was it the inseparable couple of 25-year-old miniature horses, Romeo and Juliet? Zodiac, the miracle horse who overcame all odds of surviving in the emaciated, sick state they found him? Or was it Eeyore, the cranky donkey who brayed nonstop for attention?

"Do you work with Freedom Hill Horse Rescue and Thoroughbred Placement Resources, Incorporated?" Sadie asked, since these were the two rescues she knew well.

"Yes, we do, Sadie. We try to all work together. We need each other, and many rescues fulfill a particular niche. We are the largest rescue and have years of experience in legal cases, so we end up getting a lot of large seizures of animals. State officials recognize our capacity and expertise. They call on us to testify, and know we understand the legal side of visitation, impoundment, and more. Every rescue has its purpose, and we are glad to call both those rescues partners in our larger mission, which is to look out for the well-being of all the animals. Any other questions, before I turn you loose?" Ms. Robertson asked.

"One more," Sadie said. "And it may be kind of

stupid. But I need to know. With these thousands of horses you've saved over the years, why are you making such a big deal out of me? I only saved ten horses."

"That's not a stupid question, and I'm glad you asked. You see, it may be only ten horses to you, but it's the fact you took this mission on, at your age. Consider if even one out of ten people your age did the same thing. Think about all those homes for horses."

"I guess I hadn't thought about that," Sadie said.

"Any more questions? No? All right, I'll be on my way then. I'll see you at the outdoor stage at 3 o'clock. Enjoy the rest of your day!" And Ms. Robertson left.

Times like this made Sadie question whether her calling should be in horse rescue or in equine-assisted activities. She remembered some of the harrowing and stressful experiences while trying to save the horses and her gut told her she was on the right track to try the therapy side. While she loved seeing happy endings in horse rescue, which surrounded her today, she also understood a dark side of this mission. She wasn't sure she could handle the dark part full-time. She decided instead of worrying about lifetime decisions right now, she would follow Ms. Robertson's directions and enjoy the day.

28

Surprise!

The announcement reverberated throughout the grounds: "Please join us at the outdoor stage in fifteen minutes for the Responsible Horse Ownership Day presentations and ceremony." They hadn't mentioned Sadie by name. Things were looking up.

The Navarro clan plus Katie stood at the right-hand side of the stage with a good view. The awesome band Gaelic Storm had everyone on their feet dancing and clapping to their Irish tunes. The band stopped a minute ago, but the large crowd stayed in place. Sadie should have been nervous, but she wasn't. She'd been assured she wouldn't be giving a speech, and all she had to do was go shake the senator's hand. Sadie had met a Maryland delegate, but not a senator, so she was excited about that.

While waiting, an older man who towered over Austin's six-foot frame approached them. At six feet seven inches tall, the kind-faced man wearing a summer suit peered down over his wire-rimmed glasses and said, "I understand you are the Navarros?"

Mom looked suspicious, then noted his nametag, and answered, "Why yes, we are. It's a pleasure to meet you, Senator."

"Mrs. Navarro, I'm Ed Reilly, and the pleasure is all mine. And who else is here?" he asked, gesturing to the other three.

Mom answered, "This is my son, Austin, and his girlfriend, Katie. And this is my daughter, Sadie, who is not happy about being famous today."

"Why not? Well, I'm honored to meet you. I look forward to presenting you an award today. And then I have another surprise. I wanted to make sure and invite you to my office where we can sit and chat. Today's a bit hectic, but I'd love to show you around and to get to know you better. Do you think you can do that?"

"That would be great, Senator. I would love to come visit. I brought my mom when I visited a delegate's office once, and maybe I can bring my dad to visit you."

The genial man winked at Sadie, and took her tiny hand in his giant one. He said, "That's a great idea. Time for me to get ready now — they're calling for me. I'll see you on the stage. Nice to meet you all." He departed toward the people beckoning him.

Whew, Sadie thought. *At least she now knew the surprise. She admitted it; she had been worried.*

The presentation began, and Mrs. Kathy Howe, the founder of Days End Farm Horse Rescue, discussed statistics on unwanted horses and the status of the rescue. The Executive Director, Erin Ochoa, read a proclamation from the governor on Responsible Horse Ownership Week and encouraged people to help educate the public about horse welfare issues. The Maryland Horse Council provided information on its organization, and invited people to participate in its Maryland Fund for Horses to help horses throughout the state. Finally, Mrs. Howe brought the next speaker, Senator Ed Reilly, out onto the stage.

"Hello, everyone, and thank you for having me here today to be part of this fantastic event," the senator began. "I get to do the fun part — present awards to those who made significant contributions in the field of horse rescue over the past year. I'll call your names, and please come up one at a time to receive your Governor's Certificate of Honor. I'd like to start with the first award, which is a huge round of applause for all of you who came today to support this effort."

Thunderous applause ensued, and Sadie turned to look behind her. The audience had swelled. Sadie guessed 400 people were there. From infants to senior citizens, it was refreshing to note all this support for the horses.

Senator Reilly continued his speech and began making presentations. Sadie breathed a sigh of relief as she observed people walk on the stage, take their certificates, shake hands with the senator, pose for a picture, and depart the stage. No speeches. "And last, but certainly not least, Sadie Navarro."

Sadie started to walk up to the stage, and heard Senator Reilly through the microphone. "Aw, come on, bring everyone else with you. Why not?" So the whole group walked up the steps and stood on the stage while Senator Reilly handed Sadie her official framed certificate.

Sadie stood feeling awkward, and glad her mom and Austin were with her. Maybe now they'd understand why she hated this stuff! They turned to the photographer for their posed picture, and Sadie turned back to the senator and said, "Thank you," starting to leave the stage.

"Not so fast, young lady," Senator Reilly bellowed loud enough for the entire crowd to hear.

Oh no! She'd been tricked; she knew it!

"We have one more presentation for you. But you'll have to close your eyes."

Sadie closed her eyes, and thought, *Oh, geez, what now?* Her mom's sharp cry interrupted her thoughts, and Sadie's eyes popped open.

There Dad stood in front of her, in his uniform, arms wide open. He was home. He was safe. And it was the happiest day of Sadie's life.

29

Post Surprise

The family hugged and kissed and cried and heard Senator Ed Reilly in the background. "For those of you who don't know, Lieutenant Commander Navarro has been in Afghanistan for the past year. He was due to return home in a few days, but Sadie's very convincing grandmother made sure he could be here for this ceremony today. Let's have another round of applause for this brave family."

Applause erupted from the audience. "Thank you. And now, you all can get reacquainted with each other off the stage, too," Senator Reilly said warmly. "Thank you for your service, Commander, and I look forward to seeing you soon."

"Thank you," Dad said, leaving the stage with his group.

Mrs. Howe took back the microphone and said, "This concludes our formal presentation for the day, but please stick around for the fun and festivities until 5 o'clock. Thank you all for coming, and we look forward to seeing you again."

"Grandma!" Sadie screamed, running into her Grandma Collins' arms. "How on earth?"

"Oh honey, anything's possible if you try hard enough. I couldn't have your dad missing your big day. And he was on his way home anyway. We have some pretty influential people in our Over-70 Surf Club. Just needed to ask the right people the right questions."

Sadie watched Dad roll his eyes, with his arm slung in a familiar way around Mom's shoulder. "You should see the trouble I'm in now," he said, looking down and shaking his head. "But hey, it's worth it."

"You're not really in trouble are you, Dad?" Sadie worried.

"No, sweetie, just kidding. Do you think your dear old dad lost his sense of humor?" He flashed the smile Sadie missed so much.

"No, I just wasn't sure."

"I am sure. I'm not in trouble. We were coming home in a few waves, and your tenacious grandma helped shuffle a few things. I was mad at first, but now I'm glad she did it."

"Let's go home," Austin suggested. "Unless anyone knows of any more surprises?"

Dad grabbed Mom's hand and started walking. "Not that I know of."

"Mom?" Sadie's mom asked, turning to Grandma, eyebrows raised.

"No more from me."

"Good, then let's go," Dad said, continuing to walk away. "Wait a minute, I don't even know where I'm going."

"Follow us, we'll show you, Dad," Austin said. Austin seemed more relaxed than he had been since before they dropped Dad off at the base last year.

Along the way, they ran into Ms. Robertson who said, "Good! I see you liked your surprise!"

"You knew?" Sadie asked.

"Yes, so did I keep a good secret?"

"Sure did. We're still in shock," Sadie said.

"Well, I was afraid with putting your name on the signs you might get suspicious. But your grandmother was so adamant that we needed to honor you right."

"That's right," Grandma spoke up. "My granddaughter deserves the recognition. Not just anyone can do what she did. No one's gonna slight my girl."

"It's nice to meet you in person, Mrs. Collins," Ms. Robertson said, pressing her soft hand into the spry 71-year-old's. "And you are right, we needed to honor her properly. I hope we did our part. I'm off now, but happy to see such a happy ending!"

"Thanks, and thanks for having us," Dad said, always the gentleman, as they continued toward the car.

The whole ride home the car filled with conversation and laughter and stories missed over the past year. Sadie stared at her dad, looking for changes, and she only recognized the dad she loved and missed so much while he was gone. She thought about how much she had worried, and the prayers, and the letters, and the e-mails, and how she couldn't believe it was all over.

Watching his animated talk and movements, she wondered if she still looked the same to him. She'd grown in the past year, and she didn't consider herself skinny anymore. She wondered if she looked older, or sadder, or anything different, and if he would mention it.

"How's my little girl back there?" he asked, turning to look at her.

"She's great, Dad. Maybe not so little, but couldn't be better." Sadie smiled.

"And how's Lucky?"

Silence. Uh oh. They hadn't told Dad about Lucky because they didn't want him to worry. But did she have to ruin this moment? She couldn't lie.

Mom stepped in. "He's okay. But he had a small accident. He'll be fine in a few months, but…"

"A few months? What happened?"

When no one answered, Katie spoke, "A girl who wasn't supposed to be riding him got on him and scared him. Now he has something like horse shin splints. And he can't be in the final show."

Sadie wished Katie hadn't tried to be so helpful. Dad didn't need to be bothered with all this now.

"Okay. But he'll be fine later, right? I had shin splints years ago, and I got better," Dad said.

Sadie answered, "Yes, he'll be okay. It's a minor injury, and he'll recover completely. But Dad, I'm not sure if you heard everything Katie said or not. Lucky can't be in the show."

"That's okay. There will be another show, right? I mean, as long as he's going to get better, that's what matters, right?"

"Uh huh, he'll be fine. But guess what I'm going to do?" Sadie asked, perking up.

"What's that?" Dad asked, feeding off her excitement.

"I'm going to compete in the last show riding Thor, the rescue horse Loftmar adopted! Isn't that great?"

"If it makes you happy, I'm happy," Dad said, smiling, not seeming to comprehend what this was about.

Grandma piped in, "I know that horse Thor can't be as special as Lucky, but my girl will make the best out of any situation. And the good news is, I get to stay for the show! That is, if your mom and dad will put up with me for the week."

"Mom, we want you to live with us all the time, so don't you start," Sadie's mom said.

The chatter continued the rest of the way home, while Sadie got lost in her thoughts. She was overjoyed her father was home, and her heart already felt better just by being near him. But she was surprised by his reaction about the show. She'd been working so hard to have him appreciate everything she learned over the year and how far she'd come. And from what she could tell so far, he didn't care at all.

30

Homecoming

The next days passed in a blur. Dad unpacked, and he and Mom stayed up late into the nights catching up on lost conversations. Sadie loved hearing them laugh and wished she had supersonic hearing to hear what they said when they lowered their voices. Dad slept more than usual, but Sadie imagined he'd lost a few nights' sleep during his ordeal. Mom had taken the week off of work since Dad was originally supposed to come home on Tuesday. It was fun having them both home for the first time in a long time.

Although Sadie loved school, she was happy it was summer so she could spend as much time at home as possible. She had lots of catching up to do with Dad. When the kids gathered back to school in a few weeks, they would all talk about their summer vacations. Sadie knew this week would top any of those vacations, no matter where anyone else went. Her dad was home.

Dad and Grandma visited Lucky on Sunday, and in their expert opinions, the horse would be fine. They scrutinized Sadie rubbing the cream on his splint injury, nodding and looking at each other like doctors in an operating room, agreeing she did the right thing. Feeding Lucky carrots, Dad told him he'd be back to visit him every day since they wouldn't let him go back to work yet. Dad mumbled something about mandatory time off and seemed miffed by it all. Lucky nuzzled him with his head, encouraging pets, and Dad seemed to get over being miffed.

On Monday, Grandma and Sadie went to the barn. Sadie wanted her dad to come, too, but he had been to the barn earlier to give Lucky his promised carrot. He said he needed to go for a run. Dad was an avid fitness freak, and always had been. Since Austin had picked up running in his dad's absence, this would be their first run together. Austin was taking Dad to the local park he'd discovered and been running in for the past year. Sadie understood Austin needed "Dad time," too.

At the barn, Sadie said, "Grandma, I'm going to go check in with Amanda. Can you grab my saddle from the boarder's tack room and meet me up here in the breezeway?"

"Sure can, Grandma's not useless. And I remember my way around here. See you in a minute."

Sadie checked in, getting ready for one of her extra last lessons on Thor before the show. When she didn't see her grandmother, she figured Grandma couldn't find her saddle. When she walked into the tack room, she wasn't exactly sure what she was seeing. Jimmy stood with his back to Grandma, hands in the air.

"What's going on?" Sadie asked, puzzled.

"I found this guy trying to steal your saddle, that's what's going on."

"Grandma, that's Jimmy. He boards here. And why are his hands in the air?"

"Because I told him 'hands up,' that's why. He may be a boarder, but he had your saddle in his hands."

"I can explain, if you'll let me," Jimmy said, appearing relieved to hear Sadie's sane voice after being held up.

"Jimmy, please, put your hands down, turn around, and let's talk. And I guess you've met my grandma now."

Jimmy turned around, looking flustered, and faced his attacker for the first time. "Ma'am, I'm James Wilson, or Jimmy, as most people call me. I'd be happy to explain, if you'll let me."

Sadie wanted to die, but somehow she wasn't surprised. Never a dull moment with Grandma Collins around. "Go ahead, Jimmy."

"This is a long story, so bear with me. You see, ma'am, I'm the one who was here when Rachel hurt Lucky. I don't know if Sadie gave you all the details, but Rachel kind of tricked me. Still, I consider it my fault. Rachel left right after, and I figured she at least owed Sadie an apology. Since we're out of school, I messaged Rachel on Facebook and told her so. She sent me back what I consider a pretty lame note to pass to Sadie."

Sadie asked in disbelief, "You're Facebook friends with her?"

"Well, not anymore. Not after the lame note. But anyhow, I thought if I got the saddle fixed, it might help make up for a little. And I wrote a note, which I'm not good at, and enclosed Rachel's note. I wasn't trying to steal the saddle, ma'am. I was putting it back, hoping Sadie hadn't noticed it was missing."

"You can imagine how it looked to me, can't you?" Grandma asked, looking for validation from either of them.

"Oh yes, ma'am." Jimmy answered, looking to Sadie, who choked back a giggle.

Sadie walked over to the saddle, running her hand over the tooled brown leather and reaching for the previously destroyed cinch. The polished leather and stitching looked perfect. "Wow, looks like new. I didn't know they could do that."

"I brought it to the best leather shop around and told them how much the saddle meant to you. They even did a rush job. Pretty good, huh? But they knew it was important."

"Thank you," Sadie said, still following the stitching with her fingers. "Can I see the note?"

"Sure," Jimmy fumbled with an envelope he had planned to leave on the saddle and pulled out a sheet of paper.

Sadie unfolded the sheet and read the following typed words: I'm sorry your horse got hurt when he spooked. Later, Rachel

She folded up the paper, and handed it back to him. "I meant the other one."

Jimmy's eyes shifted from Sadie to Grandma, then to the envelope, and back to Sadie. "I told you I'm not very good at notes," and handed Sadie the paper.

The handwritten note read:

Dear Sadie,
You can't imagine how bad I feel about what

happened to Lucky. I should have known better than to trust Rachel when she said you said it was okay. It seemed kinda weird, but then again you're so nice to everyone all the time that it kinda made sense, too. I thought maybe you really didn't want to let her ride your horse, but you probably didn't want to make her feel bad by telling her that. So, knowing you, I figured you would rather YOU feel bad than make HER feel bad. I hope you know what I mean.

I learned a big lesson. In the future, I will trust my gut and not try to be so cool. Especially when it comes to girls.

I think about all the things you do, and well, you're just a very different kid. I hope you can forgive me and we can still be friends.

Sincerely,
Jimmy
P.S. I got your saddle fixed for you.

"I like your note better," Sadie said, meeting his eyes and wishing her face wasn't on fire. "For Rachel, that apology was probably a lot. The whole thing was a bad accident, and I'm sorry it happened. I forgive you, Jimmy, and I appreciate you trying to make everything right."

"Thanks, Sadie," he said, looking embarrassed.

Grandma tapped her watch, and said, "Lesson...."

"Oh — sorry, you're right. I'm already behind. I have to go tack up Thor."

"I'll come help. After all, it's my fault you're late," Jimmy said, leading the way toward Thor's stall.

Following behind, Grandma whispered to Sadie, "I like this guy."

Grandma. One minute she thinks he's a criminal, the next, her future grandson-in-law.

When Sadie eventually entered the indoor ring with Thor, Jimmy said goodbye.

"And will we see you again?" Grandma asked.

"More than you want, I'll bet. Are you staying for the show on Saturday?"

"Can't wait for it. I hope Sadie doesn't have to beat you!"

"Naw, Mrs. Collins, lucky for me, we're in different divisions. But maybe next year. Who knows. See ya."

Grandma stood next to Amanda at the entry gate for the beginning of Sadie's lesson. Sadie eyed Grandma giving Amanda tips, and appreciated Amanda's smile. They didn't practice jumping today because they only focused on what they would do at the show — walk, trot, and canter. Sadie rode Thor at different speeds, and concentrated on keeping straight on the rail and deep in his corners. Amanda reminded her of her body position and told her to relax.

Before her last set of canters in each direction, Sadie caught two figures jogging down the hill to the barn — Dad and Austin. Perched against the open arena door, they watched Sadie do her thing. When Sadie halted Thor per Amanda's instruction, Sadie heard Dad clapping and hollering, "Wow! What was that? Did you run the spots right off of your horse?"

"No, Dad, this is Thor," she hollered across the ring.

"I know that. Looking good, Sadie, looking good. I'm seeing blue ribbons in your future!"

Good, Sadie thought. Maybe Dad *did* care about the show after all.

31

Final Show Prep

Sadie took her lesson on Tuesday with Miss Kristy who convinced her she looked better than anyone else ever had on Thor. Miss Kristy reminded her to keep her chest out, shoulders back, and to follow with her hands at the canter. Sadie had been taking lessons here for over a year, and she still learned something each and every time she rode. If only she could remember it all on Saturday.

At the end of the lesson, Miss Kristy said, "It's so nice to finally meet you, Mr. Navarro. I've heard a lot about you. And I have a surprise for you both."

Sadie, Grandma, and Dad looked at each other. "Surprise?" Sadie asked, remembering the last surprises.

"Yes, I've arranged for you to visit my friend's SPIRIT Program in Virginia. Sadie, you know about EA-GALA – the Equine Assisted Growth and Learning Association, and you know we do EAGALA work as part of Desire Ministries."

Sadie nodded.

"Well, SPIRIT is an equine program specifically for military families, and I expect you'll really enjoy it. Please accept this visit as my gift to you, Mr. Navarro, to thank you for your service. And for you, Sadie, as part of your continuing education."

Dad seemed embarrassed and humbled. "Is this a counseling session?"

"No, it's a demonstration," Miss Kristy assured, shaking her head. "But you may learn a thing or two. That's kind of the way it works."

"I'm not sure about this. What do you think, Sadie?" Dad asked.

"What do I think? Dad! I want to work in the horse therapy field. What do you think I think? I'd love to go!"

"Okay then. We're in," Dad decided. "When is it?"

"A week from Saturday," Miss Kristy answered.

"Sorry, guys, but I can't stay that long," Grandma said. "Guess you'll have to go without me. But I'm sure Sadie will fill me in on all the details."

"You bet! Thank you, Miss Kristy. How exciting! We'd better be going now. Thank you again, and I'll see you tomorrow for horse club!"

"Yes, and I've arranged for you and Brady to help me with the riding portion tomorrow so you can learn something new."

"Awesome," Sadie said. "I'd love to teach people how to ride. And Brady's happy to help anywhere. The kids love him."

"You're right. You've both been good role models," Miss Kristy acknowledged.

Sadie looked to her dad and her grandma. "Thanks. I've had good examples."

"That's my girl. She can do it all," Grandma said, patting Dad on the back. "She's a winner."

Sadie blushed and said, "Let's go. Can't wait to tell Mom about our trip to Virginia!"

Dad started to speak, but stopped. He glanced at Miss Kristy, then Sadie, then Thor. He sighed. "Yes, can't wait to tell Mom some horse is going to analyze me."

He smiled, but Sadie could tell something bothered him. They used to be so close. They would be again. She'd figure out the problem. Maybe it was time for another special prayer.

***

Life was getting back to normal at home. Dad kept trying to do chores he used to do and kept finding them already done. He tinkered with the cars, and took care of the yard, knowing better than to mess with Mom's gardens. He cleaned the garage, again. Dad appeared restless, and a few times a little anxious. Sadie tried not to read too much into it. But she couldn't help but flash back to Grandpa Collins. She wanted to help somehow if she could.

32

At the Final Show

The loudspeaker announced, "Jackets are excused today, jackets are excused."

Thank goodness. At 8 o'clock in the morning the thermometer already hit 88 degrees, and the announcement meant that riders could compete without wearing the extra layer of a show jacket. Sadie's clothes already stuck to her skin, and a haze hung in the thick air. The level of excitement ratcheted up a notch from the past two shows as competitors eyed each other up for the Maryland Horse Show season's final competition.

Amanda gathered the crowd and gave her day's directions. "Drink lots of water, everyone, and make sure your horses have water. It's hot and humid. I don't want anyone passing out or getting hurt. Try to stay cool. This is the grand finale, the last show of the year. All of our riders are going in with good standings. That's because you've worked hard. Don't slip now. I have faith in you, and I know you won't. But that's one of those things coaches are supposed to say.

"By now you should have the routine down pat. You understand when to be where, and who to help when. Help each other, especially today in this heat. You'll need it. The only big change is today Thor is here instead of Lucky. Jimmy, for you this means Billy doesn't need to keep his little buddy company by the arena. Thor's a pro, and he'll be fine. But thanks for helping out the last two times, and I'm sure Sadie thanks you." Coach Amanda smiled in Sadie's direction.

"Any last minute questions?"

"No," a voice from the back said. "But I'd like to say something." It was Miss Jan. "Don't forget to have fun, guys. That's why you are here. Help each other out, have fun, and stay safe."

Miss Jan normally stopped in for part of the day for the shows, but today, she and her husband Raul would be here all day. Mr. Raul hauled the horses over and back from the stable, but he left in between. Sadie learned for the grand finale, they both stayed the full day. The riders were part of the Loftmar family, and the Martins wanted to wish their extended family well at the end of the season. Sadie also hoped Miss Jan and Mr. Raul wanted to find out how their new horse, Thor, would do at his first big show since they rescued him.

Dad said, "This is serious. I had no idea. Are you nervous, Sadie?"

"No, but she used to be," Dad's new shadow, Brady, answered. "Since I started grooming for her, everything got better."

Dad reached over and straightened the groom's hat brim. "I'll bet you're right. I'm glad you were there for her. What's next?"

"Follow me, I've got the system now," Mom said. "We can't hover over Sadie, but we need to be there the second she needs us. It's an art I've perfected at these shows."

"Yes, ma'am," Dad said, clicking his heels and saluting. "Am I ever going to know what's going on again?"

"Geez, Dad, you've been home a week, chill," Austin said. Sadie couldn't decide if Austin still thought he was in charge, or if the comment made him sound more like a normal seventeen-year-old should sound.

"Okay — relax — tranquilo — got it. Now, where do we go, boss?" he asked Mom.

"Let's go get more water and hang out by the ring. It would be nice to find shade. We'll catch you in a little while, guys."

Brady looked at Sadie's dad leaving, back at Sadie, and asked, "Can I go with them for a minute? You don't need me yet, do you? I'd like to help show your dad around."

"Great idea — go on and help." She watched Brady jog off to catch up with his new hero and mentor.

While the Loftmar crowd dispersed, Sadie asked, "Jimmy, do you have a minute?"

"For you, an hour," he joked, obviously no longer embarrassed about his note.

"It's something you said — in your note...."

"I told you I don't write good."

"That's not true. But listen, this is important. I kept reading your words, and you were right. Rachel did tell me she wanted to ride my horse — here at the shows. And I said 'sure,' because I didn't want to say no. I didn't think she'd really do it. So it was my fault. I shouldn't have been a coward. I should have said, 'No, I don't want you riding my horse.' If I had, none of that would have happened."

"You're not blaming yourself now, are you?" Jimmy stepped back.

"No, not exactly. But remember how you said you learned a big lesson? Well, I did, too. And I thank you for helping me realize it."

"You're welcome?"

Sadie laughed. "Yes, it's good."

"I sure wish you were older or I was younger, because we would have made a good couple," he teased.

"Hey, my mom's five years younger than my dad," Sadie said, wondering why she'd let that escape.

"Really? How old were they when they got married?"

"I'm not sure. Old. In their twenties."

"So, if we're both still at Loftmar in ten years, let's see how it looks," he said, looking down at his fingers as if counting. He looked back up at her. "I gotta go check on Billy."

"Um, yeah, me, too, I mean, on Thor. See you later." The air got even hotter and thicker.

Sadie arrived at Thor's stall, and the usually calm, cool, and collected gray pranced and whinnied, distressed over something. "Shhh, Thor, I'm here…easy, boy." Sadie worried right away. In this heat, he shouldn't be sweating out the water he needed. Sadie went stall to stall looking for someone, and found Jessica tacking up Snickers, getting ready for her first class.

"Do you hear Thor? Has he been doing this long? It doesn't seem like him."

"You are right, this isn't like him. He just started making this noise. He's concerned about something. It can't be the show and the commotion, because he's been fine. But something is bothering him. Good thing you showed up."

Yes, better Sadie is here helping her horse than wasting time making goo goo eyes at a guy way too old for her! "He has water, he has hay, oh, and now he's pawing. I hope he's not colicking!" Sometimes stress could cause colic.

"Take him out of his stall, and walk him around. He may be a bit anxious. And just in case he is starting to colic, that's what they would tell you to do anyway."

Great. It's the grand finale. Dad is finally here. Lucky is injured, and the Steady-Eddie horse she is supposed to ride is having a fit, and may be colicking. *There's no time to stress, Sadie, listen to Jessica and take him for a walk.*

"Thanks. I'll head to the arena and see if I can find Amanda or Miss Jan. I didn't expect this. And good luck with your classes."

"Thanks. Remember, Sadie, make it look easy. You worry too much."

For someone who didn't know her well, Jessica was right. Sadie eased into Thor's stall, buckled the lead rope to his halter, and led him out. He still cried, as if trying to reach someone, and his neck arched high. His nostrils flared, and his feet danced a jig. This was not the normal Thor.

Sadie kept talking to him to try to calm him and brought him toward the show rings. Thor didn't look back toward the Loftmar horses he was leaving, so that did not appear to be a problem. What could it be? She stroked his neck while walking him and foam oozed on his coat from sweat. She had to calm him down somehow. Another long, shrill cry, crying for something she couldn't understand.

Keep walking, keep walking. Sadie had to run into someone who could tell her what to do. Now the walking seemed to be working. Thor's cries got shorter, and quieter. Good. Whatever she was doing was working.

"Sadie!" her mom called. "Come here — you're not going to believe this!"

Sadie headed in her mom's direction, and Thor pulled her there like an Iditarod dog pulling a sled. But Thor wasn't crying, so she excused his poor behavior for a second, hoping he would relax.

"Look!" Mom said. "It's Chance!" And Sadie watched Thor snort into Chance's nostrils two feet in front of her face. The horse and pony pawed and squealed, and rubbed each other's necks with their noses, grooming each other.

A little girl in pigtails and ribbons held Chance's lead rope. She looked up to Sadie and said, "They're friends," smiling and showing her missing front tooth.

"You are right," Sadie answered. Sadie hadn't seen Chance since the day of the horse rescue at the auction. Chance left on the trailer for Miss Patsy's Marlboro Horse Ranch and a happy new home.

"This can't be Sadie?" Miss Patsy's voice called. "Morgan, do you know who this is?"

The pig-tailed girl stared blankly at the girl whose horse bonded with her pony. "No."

Miss Patsy put a farm girl hug on Sadie and said, "So good to see you again! This is my daughter, Morgan, and of course you remember Chance."

"I sure do. What's he doing here? Is he in one of the showmanship classes or something? I remember he couldn't be ridden."

"It's the craziest thing. When Sue, at the ranch, adopted him, that's what she thought, too. He was to be a companion horse for Occhi. But I got to watching him out in the field, and he was as fit and active as could be. He wanted to play and run with Occhi, and I said, there's nothing wrong with the pony. So, the vet came out and took a good look at him. She gave him a clean bill of health. She couldn't find anything wrong with him, other than he was fat and lazy from not working for a while."

"That's amazing," Dad said, still watching the two horses interact so comfortably after not seeing each other for so long. Chance stomped and squealed, and Thor nipped his neck. "Ouch."

"Oh, that's their way of getting to know each other again. Have to reestablish who's in charge."

Sadie saw Mom and Dad exchange looks.

"I'm showing Chance today," Morgan said, smoothing her breeches. "It may be his first show ever, we're not sure. But he's been so good at the ranch. Mom promised if I could get him to walk and trot nice I could come to this last show of the year. I think he's the prettiest pony here, and he's definitely the most loved."

"Won't argue with you there," Sadie said.

"So who is his friend?" Morgan asked.

"I'm sorry. This is Thor. Chance and Thor were together in the holding pen for at least a few months before they both went to the auction. That was almost a year ago."

"And they remember each other?" Her young face squished up, eyes squinting.

Dad spoke up, "Sometimes when people, and animals, I guess, go through tough times together, they share a special bond. Besides, Sadie tells me horses have great memories."

"They sure do!" Miss Patsy said. "Folks, it was great running into you, but we need to get Morgan and Chance ready for their class. Take care, and good luck to you today! Bring Thor by the ranch anytime, ya hear?" Morgan patted Thor, waved goodbye, and led Chance away. The two horses stomped once again, and Chance looked over his shoulder, as if saying goodbye. The two horses seemed satisfied the other was in good hands.

"Mom, Dad, you wouldn't believe what happened, I didn't know what Thor was doing up at the stalls, and—"

"He seems fine now," Mom said. "Actually, he seems happy. Look at him."

Mom was right. How strange. Thor must have felt the need to check on his long lost friend. Now he knew where he was, and Thor was fine. Horses; how would Sadie ever know everything there was to know?

Sadie reflected again on rescue stories. Where did the story come from that Chance couldn't be ridden? Sadie was so glad he went to a loving home, and a good horsewoman like Miss Patsy kept an eye on him and questioned his diagnosis. Little Chance may be a diamond in the rough.

"I'm heading back to the stalls now," Sadie said. "The classes are moving fast, and I want to give us plenty of time to get ready. Shouldn't Austin and Grandma be here by now?"

"They're probably up there looking for you," Dad said. "Better get up there before Grandma arrests someone else," he laughed, taking Mom's hand. "We're going to watch for a while, and we'll see you soon."

One crisis averted — good. Thor acted as if nothing had happened, and Sadie was glad he was mellow again. En route to the stable area, Sadie ran into Austin and Katie. Austin said Grandma was up at the stalls, giving the other riders last minute advice. While the three stood and chatted, an intruder arrived with her large dark mare.

"Hello, Austin," Rachel called, stepping into their conversation. "And who is this?" she asked, with a disapproving gaze at the well-built gray gelding on the end of Sadie's lead rope.

"This is Thor," Sadie said, amazed at the calm in her voice.

Katie piped up, "And he's a rescue horse, and not just any rescue. Sadie rescued him. It's his first show. And she's going to win with him."

"Really? Well then, ta ta, and best of luck to you on your replacement. I am sorry about what happened to the paint horse, because he was cute. You didn't tell me how spooky he was."

"I still have him, and he's still cute. He's just injured and he'll get better." Sadie wanted to correct her about Lucky being a pinto and not a paint, among other things, but instead said, "Good luck to you, too."

Rachel walked away, with her signature hair toss.

"I don't know how you can be so nice to her after everything. I don't like that girl one bit," Katie concluded.

"I've learned a lot in the past few months. I don't know why Rachel is the way she is, but I hope one day she will get over it. She may be hiding something none of us understand."

"But—" Katie started.

"It won't help if I'm mean back to her. That just makes more problems. She is who she is and I am who I am. And after all, today is for Dad, not for me."

"But — if she hadn't pulled that stupid stunt you'd be riding Lucky, and you'd win for the year. Oops, I'm sorry, I mean, I'm not saying you can't win with Thor. Still, she just makes me mad." Katie looked over at Austin, wiping the sweat from her forehead at the same time.

"Austin tells me all the time how hard you've been working. He's super proud of you, Sadie."

Embarrassed, Sadie changed the subject and fiddled with Thor's halter. "How come you don't ride horses, Katie?"

"Because you never asked."

"Do you want me to teach you to ride, as soon as Lucky is better?"

"That would be awesome."

"You're on, then. I'm helping teach the kids now, so I'll learn what to do before I start with you. I think you'll do great. But for now, Thor and I have a show to win, so cheer us on, okay?"

"You got it. We'll find the best spot we can. Good luck – although you won't need it!" Katie and Austin left for the show arena, fanning themselves with flyers from a local vendor, attempting to chase away the heat.

* * *

Once in the arena, Sadie scanned the crowd looking for her brother and found him. He mouthed the words "I believe," and held up a forefinger representing "number one." Sadie smiled, nodded, and patted Thor's neck. She mouthed back the words, "Of course," to him. Now, let the show begin.

The class began, and Sadie breathed in and out to

calm her nerves. This was it. Dad would finally see her show. She had to do her best to make him proud. As she rounded the bend, she caught Dad's sparkling eyes, and realized he had tears in his eyes. She recognized them as happy tears, and held her own back.

Thor responded to every touch of the rein and every movement of her leg with precision. He adjusted his pace exactly as she asked, and came to the squarest halt she'd ever executed. Sadie sensed he understood the announcer's commands because he followed the directions so well. She started to get excited and realized that if he kept this up, she may even win the class. What a way to start the day that would be!

"Riders line up in the center of the ring with your numbers facing the judge, please." First class over, whew. After what seemed like an eternity, the announcer spoke, "In first place, it's Sadie Navarro on Loftmar's Mighty Thor..." Grandma whooped, and Sadie felt a sense of elation she hadn't experienced since the day Dad came home. The announcer called Rachel's name in second place, so Sadie knew the competition remained tight. As usual, Rachel found Sadie to throw some kind of barb. Sadie wondered what Rachel could say, since Sadie had won the class.

"Just lucky," she said as she passed.

Sadie urged Thor forward to catch up to Black Widow. Sadie smiled and responded, "Speaking of lucky, just for the record, my Lucky is not spooky." And she urged Thor along, who seemed happy to move away, too.

Sadie's second class went equally well, and she could tell Thor was another one of those horses who loved to show. Miss Jan cheered from the sideline and said, "You're doing great with him, Sadie. Keep doing what you are doing." She looked proud of her new rescue horse, and its novice rider in her first year of showing.

The riders once again lined up in the middle of the arena, with numbers facing the judge. Rachel squeezed her way in between Thor and the horse next to him. The announcer called the placings, and Sadie exhaled, crushed. Rachel won, and Sadie placed third. Sadie fell behind.

As they headed back toward the rail for their final class, the girl with the hair dyed to match her horse's coat said, "Now that's more like it. You know, you could have put polo wraps on Mighty Thor's legs to hide those hideous scars. But I guess your little coachy didn't tell you that, did she? Too late now, too bad — might have helped him look the part of a show horse instead of a throw away."

Sadie fumed, but found the strength to speak. "I knew Thor could have worn polo wraps, but I wanted him to be himself. I'm proud of who he is." Her mind shot back to Private Schmidt and Sergeant Silva, and how they proudly wore their battle scars. She felt their courage with her in the ring right now. She saw her dad, who looked concerned, likely because by now someone had informed him this was the evil Rachel. Sadie refocused on her last class, and the good people around her, rather than dwelling on the negative.

This was it. Everything Sadie worked for this year came down to the next few minutes, and she knew it. She wished it hadn't come to the wire like this, but here it was.

"Ring one, you are now being judged at a walk. Ring one, all walk, please," she heard crystal clear. Attention to detail, Sadie, attention to detail.

Although Sadie was supposed to stay focused on the ring, she peeked to the side once she passed the judge and took in her entourage. Mom, Dad, Austin, Grandma, Katie, Brady, Coach Amanda, Jimmy and the rest of the Loftmar riders and families, all lined up at the fence. Even her new friend, Fay, sporting a giant warm smile shouted, "Make it look easy, Mercy!" Sadie had faith in the positive thoughts coming her way and knew even if she didn't win, she had the best support crew in the place.

Thor trotted without flaw in both directions. But he had been perfect in the previous class, too, and she came in third. She had to stop thinking like that. Sadie kept her eyes and ears open, keeping good spacing between herself and the other riders. She flashed back to how nervous she'd been during the first show and remembered the riderless pony flying around the ring. *Don't think like that right now!* Sadie needed to pay attention to every single detail. And she had to believe she and Thor could win.

"Ring one, all riders canter, please. Ring one, canter."

Sadie moved her outside leg back a hair, and squeezed, while pulling the inside rein back toward her hip a tiny bit. In this head-to-head competition between Sadie and Rachel, one wrong canter lead could cost Sadie the win for the year. Thor picked up the correct lead, and Sadie breathed a sigh of relief. She steadied her lower legs on Thor's sides so he did not slow down or break his gait — another sure way to lose the class. The announcer told them to walk, and reverse directions. Sadie knew this was it.

Sadie eased Thor into his canter in the opposite direction, using the same cues. He responded like a champion. Sadie smiled and relaxed knowing she and Thor had done their best, while continuing with the steady pace. On the opposite side of the ring, Sadie spied the black mare and knew it was too late for dirty tricks in the last moments of this class. All the positivity must have worked.

The horses and riders lined up in the ring waiting for the final class of the year to be called in this division. Sadie was relieved Rachel hadn't pushed in next to her this time. Staring straight ahead, Sadie told herself no matter what happened she would be happy. Lucky learned so much from the first show to the next, and now her hero Thor carried her across the finish line.

Sadie remembered her fan club and contemplated how many ways she had grown and changed. She remembered the primary reason she decided to show was to distract her from worrying so much about Dad. She realized the finale had been her goal's navigational star, and she had completed her journey.

"We have the results from class 109. In first place, it's Sadie Navarro on Loftmar's Mighty Thor; in second place, it's Seamus Paul on Cora Lou Who; in third place, it's Paige Nagle on Dance the Blues; in fourth place, it's Rachel Vitrano, on Black Widow; in fifth place, it's J.C. McGee on Banker's Solo; and in sixth place, it's Saylor Leising on To the Moon and Back. And for the year, our champion rider is Sadie Navarro, and reserve champion, Rachel Vitrano. Congratulations, riders."

Sadie had done it. She won. She couldn't breathe.

The horses and riders left the arena and dismounted outside the gate. Mom and Dad hugged Sadie; everyone hugged Thor, and the Loftmar crowd high-fived all the way around.

Amanda looked Sadie in the eye and said, "I knew you could do it," bringing Sadie to tears. Sadie turned to wipe her eyes, coming face-to-face with her rival.

"Congratulations," Sadie said, meaning it.

"Reserve champion? You've got to be kidding me. Well, at least I didn't get beaten in front of my mother. It would have killed her see me lose to a pipsqueak like you on that ragamuffin rescue horse."

That was the final straw. Sadie's blood reached its boiling point. "Listen, Rachel, you can pick on me, but I won't tolerate you picking on a defenseless horse. And I shouldn't have let you pick on my friends before, but I did. You call me a kid, but I know more about horses and people than you do, even if you are older than me. I listen. I learn. And I change. It's something I suggest you do."

Rachel turned to leave.

"I'm still talking," Sadie continued, and Rachel stopped.

"You can go through life picking on everyone else because you think the attention will make things better. But you'll have one miserable life. I've learned from strong people and animals who decide to deal with bad situations. You think you have it so bad because you lost a stupid horse show? Or because your mom doesn't care what you're doing? What about people who can't walk, or kids who can't speak, or people who have never had anyone be nice to them in their lives until they get around horses? I've met and seen people who have real challenges in their lives deal with reality way better than you do."

"Are you finished now?" Rachel asked, looking around to see who could hear.

"No, I'm not. So, here's what I have to say to you: get help, Rachel, because you need it. Picking on other people won't get you what you need. Making other people feel bad won't make you feel better. You can't feel better about anything, until you feel better about yourself. When that happens, maybe we can be friends. But until then, you need to stop picking on my friends, including Thor. I care about my friends and my animals, and they don't deserve you criticizing them just because you don't like yourself."

Sadie stood, shoulders back, unknowingly empowered by the people she'd met over the past few months. She'd just unleashed the wisdom of Captain Vinson, the counseling of Miss Kristy, the strength of Mr. Edwards, the willingness of Lucky, the resilience of Goliath and Thor, and the strength of her new friends and acquaintances who had overcome serious obstacles in their pasts. Although angry, Sadie delivered her message with far less emotion than she felt. At thirteen, Sadie had just recommended her first person to therapy.

People stood around, made small talk, and acted as if they didn't hear. Dad's jaw still sat open.

Grandma saved the day and said, "Let's go — it's time to celebrate!" Everyone started back up toward the stalls, patting each other's backs, and reliving the show's moments.

Sadie looked back over her shoulder and saw a stunned Rachel still standing frozen in place. She felt bad for a moment, until little Brady grabbed her free hand and said, "I'm glad you stuck up for Thor."

Sadie then knew her unplanned roar was right.

33

EAGALA

The Navarro family traveled through rolling green hills decorated with occasional small stone walls appearing as if they grew there centuries ago. Sadie now understood why people loved this beautiful slice of Virginia's pie called Middleburg. Mom looked nervous; Austin looked content listening to his iPod; and Dad fixated on the road ahead while driving. The quiet bothered Sadie.

"Dad, Miss Kristy told me lots of people who come here have never been around horses. Some people can't even identify a halter. She said there's one exercise where people have to halter a horse. Sounds easy, but there's lots of stuff in the ring, and people aren't sure what to grab. And sometimes when they figure it out, they try to put the halter on upside down and sideways, and…"

"Uh huh," Dad recited, still staring straight ahead, not listening to a word she said.

"Dad," Sadie continued, "do you want me to stop talking?"

"Huh? Oh, no, please, go on. I'll do a better job of listening."

When was the last time he'd called her "punkin" or "mija," the terms of endearment he used to use all the time? He seemed so distant these days.

Mom interjected, "Sadie, why don't you tell us some of the other things you've learned about this program in your research. You know more than the rest of us about anything having to do with horses."

Dad, listening now, participated in the conversation. "Yes, sorry, I'm still not so sure about this whole horse psychotherapy thing. But since it's so important to you, I'm here. What do you think, Austin?"

"Huh?" Austin took out an earplug. "Are you talking to me?"

"Never mind, I'm sure you'd agree with me," Dad said, changing his blank expression to a smile.

"I'll put my music away. Looks like I'm missing something here."

"Good idea," Mom said, reaching over to squeeze Dad's leg, to which he forced a smile.

They pulled into Windover Farm, home of the SPIRIT Program, and the photographs Sadie had seen on the website came alive. Nestled in the foot of the Blue Ridge Mountains, 37 acres of pastures stretched as far as the eye could see. As they got out of the car, cool fresh air and a scent of fresh cut grass and wild flowers greeted them. Crickets and birds chirped accompanied by the familiar sounds of grazing horses stomping at bugs and whisking their tails to shoo flies.

Dad stood motionless staring off into the mountains. Mom came up beside him and intertwined her fingers with his, the way Sadie had seen her do so many times. Dad jumped, as if she'd woken him from a trance. And then he smiled.

"This may not be so bad after all." Sadie remembered that "Dad voice" from the past.

Two women descended from the picturesque stone house on the hill which must have had one of the most spectacular views in the state. Both women were the same height and looked as healthy as the surroundings. The long-haired brunette looked a little younger than Sadie's mom, and the short-cropped blonde, slightly older. They didn't match the picture in Sadie's mind of therapists.

"I'm guessing you are the Navarro family? Hi, I'm Donna Maglio, and this is my equine specialist, Pam Milner. Welcome to Windover Farm and the SPIRIT Program. We're very happy to have you."

Mom spoke first. "Thank you, Donna and Pam. Yes, we are the Navarros, and let me introduce everyone. I'm Liz; this is my husband, Jim, my son, Austin, and daughter, Sadie. Thank you for having us." Hands shook all around. Sadie still thought this hand-shaking ritual was a bit weird between kids and adults.

"Nice place you have here," Dad said. Sadie could tell he felt a bit awkward, as if they were observing him from a clinical view.

"Thank you," Ms. Milner said, in a lovely soothing voice which echoed the birds and crickets out there. "Why don't we go up to the barn for a few minutes, and then we'll show you around?"

The small group meandered their way up to the historic 1917 flagstone barn including a tack room, a small apartment, stalls underneath, and a discussion room. Sadie sensed Dad get nervous when they entered the discussion room, but also saw him relieved when he didn't see a therapy couch. Sometimes she knew him too well. She knew he pictured he'd be lying on the couch in front of them all while these therapists asked him probing questions. It was nothing like that.

They sat around a comfy table drinking waters and sweet teas and signed paperwork while Ms. Maglio discussed the plan for the demonstration.

"This is at your pace. We have an idea of what we'd like to do. But we're flexible. Here at SPIRIT Program we use the EAGALA Model, which means the Equine Assisted Growth and Learning Association Model. We use a team of an equine specialist, in our case, Ms. Milner; a licensed mental health specialist, me; and at least one horse. The horses are the real therapists; we're just the ones who can speak."

Sadie was glad Ms. Maglio wasn't using psychological words. Dad wouldn't like that. She and Mom worked hard enough to convince him to come here today. Sadie feared if this conversation hadn't gone well, the trip may have been a waste of time. So far, from reading Dad's body language, things looked okay.

"Miss Kristy, who I work for at Desire Horse Club does EAGALA work, and talked to me about it. I thought it was so cool. I think that's why Miss Kristy 'phoned a friend' to set us up to do this, especially since you specialize in veterans and their families."

"That's right. I keep forgetting we have a professional in the crowd," Ms. Maglio joked. "Good, well, we're going to do an activity and talk about it. But I'm going to tell you a few more things about the horses and the process. We want you to understand how and why it works. So your demonstration will be a bit unique. We want Sadie to become such a fan of EAGALA that she will want to join the ranks someday."

"We'll probably reveal more of what happens be-hind-the-scenes than we would in a normal session, since this is a demonstration, not a true therapy session," Ms. Milner added.

Sadie read the relief on Dad's face from ten feet away.

"Commander Navarro, we hope if you like what we do, you will remember our services for other col-leagues. We're proud to say that we have helped a lot of people, but we can only help those who know we exist."

Mom and Dad both started to speak at the same time, and Dad stopped. Mom looked around at everyone and said, "Let's get started. What are we waiting for?"

"We were waiting for you to give the order, Mom," Dad said.

Sadie beamed when Dad gave her their special thumbs-up sign. He was going to be a good sport after all.

34

Life's Little Obstacles

The family and the EAGALA specialists wandered down the small dirt road that split the green pastures in half. There wasn't another house in sight, and the mountains hung low in the background. Fluffy white clouds in the distance appeared as if someone painted them there.

Ms. Maglio said, "When walking here with clients, we normally talk, trying to get a sense of how things have been since their last session. If it's someone's first visit, we ask how they are doing that day. The setting here relaxes people."

"I can understand why," Austin said, taking in the mountain air. "Katie sure would love it here."

"Katie is Austin's girlfriend," Sadie offered, for some reason, not annoyed with him for mentioning her today. Maybe she wasn't so bad.

"You should bring her sometime," Ms. Milner

said. "There's a very interesting dynamic with horses and couples. With couples, the horses react most dramatically. It is amazing how they pick up on underlying tension or other issues that couples themselves don't see."

The group arrived at a large outdoor sand arena filled with interesting and colorful objects — poles, brushes, halters, lead ropes, buckets, cones, jump standards, and three horses. The horses looked at them as they entered the ring and shifted positions, but none seemed alarmed.

"So, before we get started, I have a question for each of you. What would you like to accomplish today?" Ms. Maglio asked.

"That's easy; I'll go first. I want to learn about EAGALA horse therapy," Sadie started.

"Yeah, me too." Sadie shot Austin a look. He'd been playing along pretty well up until now.

Mom clasped her hands in front of her at her chest. "Ever since Sadie came home raving about her volunteer work with the kids, I've been fascinated to see how horses help. So, I'd like to participate in the demonstration and see for myself. Is that good enough of an answer?"

"Yes, of course. And Commander, how about you?" Ms. Maglio asked.

"Since now I know for sure this isn't about me being analyzed, I'd like to have some fun with my family. Away from the normal stuff. And to learn something, too. I know Sadie's learned a lot from being around horses."

Sadie wondered what her Dad meant. But she was glad the only useless answer had been her brother's "Me, too" response. Okay, so he couldn't be her perfect brother all the time.

"Thank you. I hope you will find the growth and learning part represented by the G and L in our association's name interesting. So let's get started. First, I want you each to go stand by the horse out here that most represents you in this family."

Sadie eyed up the three horses and decided the black pony with the big brown eyes and a fluffy mane looked like the baby of the group, similar to her rank in the family. She approached the pony with cautious steps, and the pony took a step toward her as she got closer. Sadie reached slowly for her neck, and scratched the same spot Lucky enjoyed having scratched. The pony turned her neck toward her new friend, asking for more. Sadie liked her choice of horse, and looked to find out how the rest of her family chose.

Austin headed toward a tall graceful dark horse, almost black, which flared its nostrils as he approached and raised its head in alarm. Austin clucked at the horse, and made soothing sounds, which helped the flaring nostrils, but not the head. As he took two more steps toward it, the horse backed. Her brother exhaled and turned around, with his back to the horse. He took a tiny step back, and stopped and waited. Since the horse did not back farther away, he did this again and again until he was right next to it. The horse sniffed him and let out a sigh, allowing him to stay.

Sadie wondered if Mom would go to the pony with her, which Sadie now figured out was a mare. But Mom didn't. Both Mom and Dad approached the largest horse in the ring, a giant bay gelding which looked to be part warmblood or draft horse. Sadie questioned why her petite mom thought this big strong horse most represented her, but figured she would find out later. The large horse did not seem to mind their presence at all, and her parents each took up their positions on either side of him while he continued to forage for something in the sand.

"Good," Ms. Milner said. "Now, if we were in a real session, we would ask questions about your choices of horse, and we would learn something right there. It's one of the beauties of the program — the immediacy. Let me talk for a minute about a question we always get: why horses for this kind of therapy? There are so many reasons, but let me share a few of them with you.

"First, no other animals have the same mirroring effect as horses, meaning they will mirror humans' emotions. Second, they are not judgmental or biased. And third, they live within a social structure, their herds, much the same as we do. We've also found by working with such large animals, they can be real confidence boosters when people find ways to get them to do things they want them to do. That can be something as simple as picking a hoof."

"Just like what you talked about at the horse club, Sadie, when Brady made one of the students feel better because he picked the hoof right for the first time." Mom seemed proud to offer something.

"Yes, and horses are very in the moment," Ms. Milner continued. "They teach people to be in the moment, even though people have a past, and a present, and a future."

"Now, moving to our exercise," Ms. Maglio said. "You see these objects in the arena, right? I would like each of you to pick a point, and build an obstacle with a few of these objects. The obstacle should represent an obstacle you are facing now. The object is to get the horse you have chosen over, through, or in and out of that obstacle. Now, as in life, you must follow certain rules: 1) No touching the horses, 2) No bribing them with food, and 3) You can't use anything outside of your community, which is this arena. We normally also say 'no talking,' but since this is a demonstration, you can talk today. Any questions?"

Sadie asked, "Can we know the horses' names?"

Ms. Milner answered, "Yes, since you asked. The pony you are scratching, her name is Midnight. Austin, you have paired up with Demitasse, or Demi, as we call her here. And Commander and Mrs. Navarro, your gelding is Tapdance, or Tappy. Any other questions?" She looked from person to person. "Good, then go ahead and get started."

Sadie thought first about an obstacle she faced now. Pretty much the biggest obstacles she had been facing were her fears about Dad, worrying about working with the veterans, and the big show. All those were over now. She decided to start collecting items to build an obstacle, and figure out what it meant later.

Gathering four poles, Sadie laid them in a square on the ground. She would get the pony to walk into the box, stop, and then walk out the other side. This obstacle would have been easy with a halter and a lead rope. Without touching Midnight, Sadie figured it would be a challenge. But she was up for it.

Sadie watched her parents while they each built an obstacle. Dad, a construction battalion engineer, seemed to find this a fun project. Sadie laughed inside wondering how complicated he would make this, and remembered the first tree house he built for her when she was five. He built a rope ladder up the side to reach a boat-shaped platform and installed a working wooden ship's wheel. She played in that tree house for hours taking imaginary adventures on the high seas. Even Austin humored her and came along for nautical journeys. Sadie hadn't thought about the tree house for years, and wondered why it came to her now.

Fortunately, Dad did not build a tree house for the horse to climb, but lined a series of cones in a zigzag pattern. Three cones on each side of a channel in one direction, then two buckets on each side; three cones on each side at an opposite angle, then two more overturned buckets. He spaced the cones symmetrically, and everything stood neat in place. Sadie's dad liked things this way, everything neat, in place, and in balance. He paced off his cones one more time to ensure the correct spacing, and looked up to see what Mom built.

Mom's creative side came out. She lined two poles up on the ground creating a chute, and at the end she lined up a series of brushes, fluffy side up. Most horse people wouldn't use brushes as part of an obstacle, but it worked. Sadie already imagined the horse looking down at the brushes on the ground, wondering what they were doing there. But Sadie remembered in her reading that EAGALA wanted people to figure out things for themselves, so she didn't interfere. Besides, Mom had ways of making amazing things happen, so she didn't doubt her or her weird brush line.

Austin's obstacle was simple. He created a small jump — one pole on two jump standards. She knew he'd seen these at the barn, and at the shows and watched many horses hop over them. Sadie thought okay, Austin, easy with a rider. She wondered how he would get what appeared to her to be a bit of a diva of a thoroughbred horse over the jump without touching her.

Now with obstacles built, Ms. Maglio surprised Sadie, by saying, "Sadie, why don't you go first." She didn't ask what the obstacle meant, which relieved Sadie, because she still wasn't sure.

Sadie nodded, and approached the pony like she had the first time. Midnight once again took a step toward her as she got close. Maybe she'd remembered Sadie scratching her neck and wanted more. Sadie remembered the "no touching rule," but bent over playfully, nose to nose with the tiny mare. With ears up, Midnight sniffed Sadie's face, whiskers tickling her and causing a small laugh. Sadie pulled her face back an inch, saying, "Good girl, pony kisses, right?" And she giggled again.

Sadie got close enough to breathe through her nose gently into the pony's nostrils. Sadie knew this was how horses got acquainted with each other. She did it with Lucky all the time, and recently, with Thor. The pony pulled her head back a few inches, and stretched her neck forward again, asking for another sniff of this strange smelling two-legged horse. Sadie breathed out again, and the pony nudged her with her nose. Midnight breathed out through her large nostrils into Sadie's face. Sadie smelled the green grass the mare had been chewing, and decided she'd made a friend.

Turning her back to Midnight, Sadie took three steps toward her box outlined on the ground with poles. Sadie heard pony footsteps right behind her, and the small furry nose brushed her elbow. Encouraged by Midnight, Sadie stepped right over the pole into the center of the box and stopped. Her equine companion followed her. Sadie turned to face her and wanted to hug her so badly, but the rules said she couldn't. The mare looked at her through long black eyelashes and pawed the ground. Midnight threw her head back, bumped Sadie's hand looking for a caress or a treat, and stomped. Sadie felt terrible, the pony had done exactly what she'd asked her to do, and she couldn't reward her.

Sadie spoke to her softly, remembering her voice was one of her natural aids. "There, good girl. You don't understand, but once we're out of this box and our exercise is over, I can love you all I want. So let's go, okay?" Sadie felt so foolish that tears were welling up in her eyes because she couldn't pet this pony. She was thirteen now, not three! She hoped no one could see. Walking out of the stupid box she created, the pony followed. Sadie turned to find Ms. Maglio and said, "That's it."

"Good job, Sadie. Way to start us out. Now, who wants to go next?"

Sadie threw her arms around Midnight's neck, scratched her withers, and made a big deal out of her. The pony seemed to be trying to groom Sadie back, moving her head back and forth, against her body.

"I'll go," Sadie's mom said right away.

Ms. Maglio nodded. Sadie's mom, standing by the giant bay horse, grabbed the hot pink plastic hula hoop. Sadie's dad moved away from the other side of Tappy, and stood closer to his zigzag cone construction site.

"Shoo, shoo, go now," Mom said, waving the hula hoop toward the horse's behind to try and get him to move forward. The horse turned to look at her, but didn't budge. Mom moved to the other side of the horse and tried it again, this time adding clucking noises. Mom did this at various positions around the horse. No progress.

Sadie saw her mom getting frustrated. "Mom, do you want me to try to help?"

"No!" Mom said at once, and a little too loud. "I mean, I think that's against the rules."

"No. I think it's allowed. Ms. Maglio, Ms. Milner?" Sadie asked, desperately wanting to help her mom.

"What are the rules, Mrs. Navarro?" Ms. Milner asked.

"No touching, no bribing, and don't use anything outside of something," Mom answered.

"Outside of your community, or the arena. I'm in your community, Mom."

"Well then, yes, okay, you can help. Thank you for the clarification. Somehow I thought this would be easier," Mom said, embarrassed.

Sadie joined her mom, and they talked for a minute. They decided they would try to pull the horse through the chute rather than push him. Sadie suggested Mom pick up a brush from the end and let Tappy sniff it. Then Mom should walk backwards, holding the brush out, hoping the horse would follow the brush out of curiosity or the scent. Sadie would walk alongside the horse and help guide her mom straight through, since she'd be walking backwards.

Mom chose a brush, and eased it under the giant nose. The horse reacted, pulling his head back and snorting out. Loudly.

"What now?" Mom asked, dropping the brush to her side.

"Let's try another brush. He may not like the horse whose scent is on that particular brush. Remember, horses are sensitive."

Sadie's mom cocked her head and raised her eyebrows in a you've-got-to-be-kidding-me look, which made them both laugh.

Mom went to the brushes, picked up another one, sniffed it, looked at Sadie, shrugged her shoulders, and said, "Maybe this one is friendlier." Sadie was glad her Mom's sense of humor had returned.

Approaching the horse again, Sadie's mom repeated her action with the brush, and this time Tappy came closer. He investigated the brush, sniffed it, and approved the scent. Mom said, "Now we're getting somewhere."

Mom took a step back toward the chute, holding the brush out, and the horse followed. Another step back and he followed again, licking his lips. Sadie realized these were the only steps this horse had taken since they entered the arena. She walked alongside, clucking, and letting him know what a good boy he was being. The horse looked in her direction, but focused again on Mom's eyes and the brush, paying no attention to the poles on the ground, she led him through.

"Mom, you're going straight, but you are almost to the brushes. Keep walking backwards as if they weren't there. Hopefully he will follow. I think he will." Oops, she realized she probably wasn't supposed to say this because Mom was supposed to be figuring things out for herself. But Sadie couldn't help it, it was true. And Mom looked so happy to be winning this game.

Mom looked down and stepped backwards over the brushes. The big horse stopped as he reached the line, with Mom on the other side. He dropped his head to the ground, sniffed one. Then he sniffed another, then another, on down the line. He looked up at Sadie's mom and confirmed Sadie's earlier fears. The horse had never seen brushes on the ground in a line, and he didn't trust his leader enough to walk over the strangeness.

And Sadie had just told her mom she thought Tappy would do it.

Mom talked to the horse. "It's okay. You don't like some of those brushes. But at least you didn't run away from them. How about if I make them go away?" Mom continued to hold the one brush up in one hand. She bent over and reached down with the other hand. She pushed the brushes, one at a time, out of the horse's path. She cleared enough brushes away so he could walk through without having to step over them and then she stood up straight again with confidence.

"Now there, better, right? The horse looked down again, back up to her, and she held the brush closer to his nose again. She stared into his big soulful brown eyes, and said, "C'mon, we can do this together," in a soft, inviting voice. She took one step back, and he followed, and another step back, and whether consciously or not, licked her lips. The two traveled in unison until all four of Tappy's feet passed the brush line. "Good boy!" Mom yelled, and threw her arms around the startled horse's neck. She didn't wait for the facilitators to tell her it was okay.

"Well done, Mrs. Navarro," Ms. Milner said, and Austin and Dad gave a small clap. Mom bowed, and gestured to her horse partner, sharing the credit.

Mom walked over and kissed Sadie on her forehead. "Thank you, my little horse whisperer." Sadie was glad to see her mom happy, but wished she would give herself credit for her work.

"I'll go next," Dad said, "unless you want to go next, Austin."

"No — have at it, Dad." Austin's mare took a liking to him. Wherever he moved, she stayed right beside him.

Mom walked over to Dad's obstacle and delivered the large horse, who followed her now. "Thank you," he said.

Dad hollered over to the facilitators, "So you don't want to know what my obstacle is?"

"No, we'll get to that later."

"Okay, well, here goes." Dad had a lead rope in his hand, and threw the end of it toward the horse's hind legs, moving him away. "Easy boy, you'll be fine. I'm not going to hurt you," he said, but Tappy didn't look like he believed him. As Dad moved the lead rope toward him again, the horse pinned his ears back, and he kicked toward the rope. "Hmmm…you don't like that. Sorry, guess my Texas roots came back, and I was trying to be a cowboy. Let's try something else."

Dad looked at the objects in the arena and picked up the brushes his wife had discarded. He brought them back to his site, and placed them behind the horse. Tappy turned around and looked down at them. His tail swished, and Sadie wondered if he would kick out at them, too. Dad looked at the hula hoops, and may have considered Mom's attempt with those because he didn't choose them. He picked up a pole and tapped the ground behind the horse, sending him flying across the arena in a gallop toward Austin and the mare.

The mare startled, too, when Tappy took off. She ran behind Austin seemingly for protection. Austin waved his hands above his head as the big bay horse came close, and he snorted and turned with his back end toward Austin and Demi. The mare whinnied, and the bay gelding snorted again. Sadie noticed the little black pony went to join the group, keeping her distance, but still closer to the herd of horses than the herd of humans.

Dad asked Mom for the brush, which she clutched right now. "I'll see if this works." He brought the brush over to Tappy, trying to get his attention with it. The gelding sniffed it and trotted off in the opposite direction. Sadie couldn't understand what was happening because her dad was so good with animals. They loved him. Sadie regretted talking her dad into this now. If she was in Dad's position, she'd be humiliated. Dad tried a few more times, with the same results.

"Ms. Maglio and Ms. Milner, are you considered to be in my community?" Dad asked.

"Yes, Commander, we are."

"Great, then can you help me, please? I don't want to waste everyone's time here while I chase this horse around and wear us both out."

"Isn't that cheating?" Mom asked. And she wasn't kidding.

"Geez, Mom, they said it was in the rules," Austin said, coming to Dad's defense. "But Dad, why didn't you ask Sadie? You saw what she did with her pony, and you saw what she did with Mom."

"Look, it's hard enough for me to ask for help at all. And you are my children. I'm the one who is supposed to be helping you, not the other way around."

"But you didn't mind asking me to help you while you were gone." Austin looked Dad in the eye across the arena.

How strange to hear Austin challenge anyone but Sadie.

"You know, you're right." Dad turned his attention and gaze to the gathered herd of horses. "But maybe I asked too much. For now, let's just get through this demonstration, because we still have your turn to go," Dad said, looking defeated.

Ms. Milner started, "Commander, what is it that the horse seems to like the least?"

"Me," Dad said, finally with a smile.

"Think about it," she coaxed.

Sadie could tell her dad was concentrating. He pointed to areas in the arena in which things happened, reliving the situation in his mind. "He doesn't like things happening behind him."

"And when does he seem most relaxed?" Ms. Milner continued.

"When he has eye contact, and is following."

"So why don't you work with that for a few minutes, and let's see what happens."

Dad approached Tappy, ensuring the horse could see him the whole time. Dad began to back up, and the horse took a step forward. Dad looked down, and then back into Tappy's eyes. The horse mirrored his actions, looking down at the steps, then back in the eyes. Dad shot a glance over at Sadie and smiled. He backed the horse to the symmetrical cones. Although cautious, the horse followed him. Dad looked thrilled, until he reached the bend in his course. The horse looked down, and didn't seem to understand.

"Liz, can you come over here, please?" Dad asked Mom, who showed up by his side. "Do me a favor, and walk alongside him in the same spot Sadie did, so we can help him understand this bend in the course. He trusts you already, just move slowly, and don't get behind him."

"Sure," Mom said. She still looked at Dad the way Katie looked at Austin.

Mom moved to Tappy's side where he needed to turn. She kept getting closer, and Tappy would take a side step away. When his body was in the right position, Dad continued with his earlier ritual and backed the rest of the way through the course, with Mom working alongside. At the obstacle's end, Dad shouted across the arena, "Got it! Thanks to everyone else!"

Sadie wondered why Dad had such a difficult time taking credit for things, too. But her dad looked elated with the success.

"Last but not least," Austin said. "Mine's going to be easy." Austin took a few running steps toward his jump and leaped over it, expecting Demi to follow. He looked back, and her ears moved back and forth, paying attention, but she did not follow.

"Okay, how about this?" Austin stood in the same place, still facing her, on the other side of the jump. He made kissing noises at her and said, "Come on, you can do it, c'mon, pretty girl."

The mare arched her neck, walked a step, and trotted a few steps toward him, while Austin grinned ear to ear. Two feet before the jump, she veered to the left and went around the jump to join her kissing-noise friend on the other side. "So close!" Austin said, moving to stroke her. He pulled his hand back at the last minute, probably remembering the rules.

"I have an idea," Dad said. "Why don't I come and stand on that side of the jump to keep her from going around it?"

"I guess that's allowed, huh?" Austin asked, looking toward the facilitators, who nodded together. "Thanks, Dad. Hopefully that will work." Austin walked back toward their starting position, and the diva mare followed. Dad stood at the left side of the jump, and the mare eyed up Dad as a competitor to her new friend's attention. She drew closer to Austin, who reached to pet her again and caught himself. Austin started with the running jump again, got to the other side, and called her again.

This time, Demi started right off in a trot. Keeping a close eye on Dad, she cleared the jump by at least two feet higher than necessary. Demi landed next to Austin and halted. Snorting, the mare looked back at Dad and then rubbed her head on Austin's shoulder. Austin reached up and gave her the reassuring pets she needed. "Good girl, way to go. And thanks, Dad."

"Happy to be of some use," Dad said.

"Austin, since you went last, let's start with you," Ms. Maglio said. "What obstacle did the jump represent?"

"I guess now is as good a time as any to talk about it. I've been thinking of joining the Navy."

Sadie heard her mom gasp from across the arena, and Sadie's own heart sank. Not that she wouldn't be proud of her brother, but she couldn't imagine him moving away from the family or being away like Dad had been.

Austin continued, while patting Demi's neck. "I actually tried to join, but since I'm seventeen, I needed my parents' permission. I thought about trying to tell Mom that Dad said it was okay, and telling Dad that Mom said it was okay. But I guessed they would figure it out. I had a friend who did that with his mom and his long-time mentor and family friend, and it worked for him. But those two weren't married. So I thought my case might not work as well. So I didn't try."

"So what did the horse do regarding this obstacle?" Ms. Milner asked.

"You know, I thought since she seemed so attached, she would just follow me. So it surprised me when she went around the jump. I mean, she still got to me, but in her own way."

"And why do you think she went over the second time?"

"I think she wanted to do the right thing. And

with Dad there, it was that extra help she needed to go over and not around."

"Do you think having your dad there helped her make the right decision?"

"Yes, I do. And maybe that's some kind of 'sign' as my grandma would say, that I should be waiting for the right time for such a big decision."

"Or at least talk to people about it," Sadie said, in a low quiet voice.

"Now that Dad is back, and I'm freed up from being the man in the family, I can do that. But really, maybe I can just be a kid again, and keep thinking about it. When the time comes, I'll know. And I will talk to everyone," Austin finished, looking straight into Sadie's hurt eyes.

"Commander Navarro, how about you?"

"That will be a tough one to top. Wow. Mine is hard to explain, but it's kind of like getting my role back in the family. Everyone seems to have replaced me."

The family exchanged looks, in silence.

"I mean, even in here. We go to pick a horse, and Mom and I both go choose the biggest horse. And then she makes him work better than I can. At home, everyone has their chores, their routines, and I feel in the way — like a stranger," he said, looking at Tappy. "Everything's changed."

"How did you get the horse to respond to you, Commander?"

Dad thought, and a smile spread across his face. He again pointed to the areas in the arena where his interactions with Tappy took place. "This is crazy. I stopped pushing from behind and gained his trust by communicating with him — up front — looking into his eyes. I think I see what you mean here. How did you do that?"

Ms. Maglio responded, "We didn't do anything. It's what the horses do — with you."

"Except you helped."

"We helped because you asked for it. That's the hardest step for most people. I hope you'll remember that and pass that along when needed," Ms. Maglio said, with conviction.

"And Mrs. Navarro, what did your obstacle represent?" Ms. Maglio asked. Sadie wondered, too.

"Mine seems minor compared to those two, but it's important to me. I started what, in my opinion, is the most important job I've had in my life, well, outside of being a mom," she smiled. "The kids have become so self-sufficient, and we have been working it out so well. And now, well.... I just don't know if there's going to be enough of me to go around to be a mom, a wife, and a full-time worker in a high-stress important job. And I worry about that."

"So what did the horse do?" Ms. Milner asked.

"I realized he didn't want to budge when I asked him to move from behind or the sides. With Sadie's help, I got him to follow me. But he didn't want to follow at first, because he didn't like the first brush. But when I got the right brush, he followed. And with my helper at the side, and him keeping an eye on her, too, we made it through the first part."

"Why do you think he did that?" the equine specialist asked again.

"The first choice I made wasn't the right one, so I readjusted. And he began to trust me. Also, with Sadie helping guide me, I didn't walk him into any poles, which he probably appreciated."

"What happened when he stopped at the line?"

"Again, I thought for a minute about just making him go over it, or asking Sadie to help me get him over it with her horse magic. But I realized it was my obstacle, and I built it. So maybe a better way to make it work was a compromise. So I moved the brushes from right under his feet, but I still made him cross the line and finish. And it worked!" Mom answered.

"So there may be a metaphor here to what's happening with the change in your life and your family and at work," Ms. Maglio suggested.

Mom closed her eyes for a second, opened them again, and studied her obstacle on the ground. "You mean maybe we'll need to make some adjustments — not just in the family, but at work. See what works, and what doesn't, to get across that line."

"For many of these sessions, people take with them what they learned today and use it in the weeks to come. But yes, that seems to be a good interpretation — adjustments," Ms. Maglio said.

"And how about you, Sadie? Tell us what happened out there with you and Midnight."

"Honestly, I built the obstacle, but I wasn't sure what it represented. I feel like I've had a bunch of big things on my mind, and most of them have gone away right now. I still want Lucky to get better from his injury, but that's not really an obstacle. So I built something for the pony to go through, but wasn't sure what it was. Is that normal?"

"Why don't you walk us through what happened, and maybe the horse can help you figure it out," Ms. Milner said.

Sadie walked over to her obstacle so she could physically walk through it to remind her. Midnight showed up at her side again; Sadie reached over and scratched her little buddy. "I breathed into the pony's nose because I knew that's how horses greet each other. I was glad that made her follow me so easily."

Sadie reenacted the few steps into the box, and Midnight followed again. Sadie stopped and looked into the pony's expectant eyes. This time Sadie rewarded her with a strong scratch behind her left ear.

"But when I got to the middle, I felt so bad because I couldn't pet her. And she didn't seem to understand that. It was kind of ridiculous, but I thought I was going to cry."

"What did she do to make you think she felt so bad, Sadie?" Ms. Milner asked.

"Because she pawed the ground and stamped her feet, like she needed attention."

The two facilitators looked at each other, and Ms. Milner spoke up, "We have to tell you, Sadie, that was very unique. We have never seen her do that. What do you think she was trying to say?"

Sadie looked the shiny black pony in her big beautiful eyes and scratched behind both ears, thinking about it. "What were you trying to tell me?" Sadie's eyes welled up again when she realized the answer.

Slowly, methodically, she spoke the words she had not been able to say until now. "She wanted me to be proud of her." Sadie choked back more tears, as she realized she was no longer talking about the pony. Sadie was talking about herself.

"I think she felt like me, like I've felt since the final show. Like I've felt since Dad came home. I worked so hard while he was gone and dedicated myself to doing well in the horse shows so my dad would be proud of me.

But the show happened, and I won — grand champion for the whole year — and I couldn't even finish the season on my own horse. And he didn't care." By now, she sobbed.

Dad came to her side, took her hands from the pony, and turned her to face him. He placed his hands on her shoulders and asked, "Why would you think I'm not proud of you?" Sadie heard and saw Dad's hurt at the same time.

A waterfall of words and tears gushed at the same time, while Sadie struggled to maintain some kind of composure. "The show, Dad, you didn't make a big deal at all, and it was a big deal to me. And since you've been home, I've been an afterthought. You haven't even asked me to go out to find our favorite Chinese restaurant which we always do, and you said you would do in our e-mails and letters. It was my first year of showing, and I was scared to death, but I did it for you, Dad. And you didn't even seem to notice." She stopped, her chest heaving, taking in gulps of air.

The rest of the onlookers watched in silence, including the horses. Midnight turned to join the other two horses, perhaps realizing her job was done.

Dad looked at Sadie with surprisingly sad eyes. "I am so sorry, Sadie. I would have never imagined you would think I wasn't proud of you. I'm sorry if I didn't get as excited about the show as you expected. But Sadie, to me, it's not about the show."

Dad pulled out the hanky he always had in his back pocket, unfolded it, and handed it to Sadie. "I'm proud of you for your partnership with Thor, your ability to go with change, the things you do for other people — these are the things I admire about you Sadie, not the blue ribbons. I know you worked hard, and I am proud. But I am prouder of who you are inside, not how good you became at showing a horse. I've always believed in you, and knew you could do whatever you set out to do."

Sadie dabbed her eyes and wiped her nose.

"Look at the lives you've touched — horses you've saved — people you've encouraged. Yes, you are my winner, but it's not about the show ring. What I saw in you at the show was the determined daughter I know I have who worked hard to win. What I saw after the show is the person I always hoped you would become.

"In one of the proudest moments of your life, rather than enjoy the attention, you stood up to a bully who picked on a helpless animal and your friends. That is the Sadie I couldn't be any prouder of, and I'm sorry if I haven't shown that well. Things have changed, everyone has grown, and sometimes I'm not sure where I fit. The horse reinforced that for me today. But one thing is for sure, I never meant to hurt you. And I'm so sorry if I did."

When Midnight got close to Demi and Tappy, Demi squealed and kicked out at her, trying to keep her away from Tappy. Ms. Milner asked the group, "Did you see that?"

The family nodded, still appearing stunned from Sadie's emotional discussion with Dad.

"Sadie, you know horses. Why do you think that happened?" Ms. Milner asked.

"Because I'm upsetting them by standing here crying like a baby?"

"True, they do feed off of our emotions, but what else?"

Austin said, "I know. Can I answer?"

"Go ahead," Ms. Maglio encouraged.

"Horses are herd animals, and they are regrouping as a herd. So, they are trying to prove their positions in the herd. Even though they all know each other, they need to be reminded of who is who, because something may have happened when they were gone that makes them different when they get back."

"That's right. And this happens with people, too. Sometimes they need to get reacquainted. And talking is a great place to start," Ms. Maglio said.

Mom and Austin joined Sadie and Dad, still standing in the box lined by poles on the ground. They hugged all around like they hadn't since before Dad left.

Dad said, "Thank you, ladies, and horses. I think we've learned a lot here today."

Sadie thought about it, and thought about everything that had happened in the past few months. The reasons for many events weren't clear to her at the time. She found that facing fears enriched the soul, and that winners come in many shapes and sizes. Her family had grown; she had grown; and she discovered more about herself and others through her experiences. And she no longer harbored her fearful secret.

She experienced the healing power of horses.

She discovered the joy of helping others.

She made her dad proud.

And yes, she believed once again, everything happens for a reason.

Acknowledgments

Thank you to my husband, Jaime, for continuing to believe in me. I could not have written this book without his love and support. Color me lucky! Thank you, too, to my mom, Flo, and my brother, Eddy, who both provided valuable advice and perspectives. I've been so fortunate to have these wonderful influences in my life.

I would like to acknowledge military veterans and families of today and yesterday. Thank you to my military mentors who instilled many of the principles relayed in this book and inspired certain characters. I can't say enough about the strength of our military service members.

I thank the people and organizations that educated me and helped me accurately portray equine assisted activities and therapies. Maryland Therapeutic Riding, Caisson Platoon Equine Assisted Programs, Desire Ministries, Equine Assisted Growth and Learning Association, and the SPIRIT Program all spent valuable time to help me develop this story. Mary Jo Beckman, Kristy Alvarez, Donna Maglio, and Pam Milner -- you all demonstrate how horses help people in your own dedicated ways.

Thank you, Loftmar Stables, for teaching me lessons in horsemanship, sportsmanship, and horse showing that I can share with others. Jan and Raul Martin, you leave a legacy in the state of Maryland for the thousands you have touched. I would be remiss if I did not mention the valiant horse rescue efforts of Freedom Hill Horse Rescue, Thoroughbred Placement Resources, Inc., and Days End Farm Horse Rescue. You horse savers, and the animals you serve, continue to be heroes!

Thank you to my copy editor, Joyce Gilmour of Editing TLC, for her dedication, professionalism, and interest in this book. And finally, I thank my publisher, J.B. Max Publishing, for bringing a second "Believing In Horses" story to the world.

Website links to all organizations listed in "Believing In Horses, Too" are available at www.believinginhorses.com.

Valerie Ormond

 Valerie Ormond served a career in the U.S. Navy before beginning her second career as a writer. Her first novel, "Believing In Horses," won the Military Writers Society of America Gold Medal for Young Adult Books; the Gold Medal for Children's Literature in the Stars and Flags Book Awards; the Parent Tested Parent Approved Best Product and Official Winners Seal of Approval; and additional awards and recognition.

Valerie's nonfiction articles have appeared in numerous books, newspapers, and magazines. She holds memberships in writing organizations including American Horse Publications, the Military Writers Society of America, the Society of Children's Book Writers and Illustrators, and the Accokeek Women Writers Group.

She is the founder and Chief Executive Officer of Veteran Writing Services and a member of the first National Women Veterans Speakers Bureau. Valerie is a lifetime member of the Naval Intelligence Professionals and Disabled American Veterans, and strongly supports military and veteran families. She also owns and rides horses and has served as Secretary of the Maryland Horse Council, an organization representing 30,000 horse people. She lives in Maryland with her husband, Jaime Navarro.

Author contact information:
www.believinginhorses.com
www.veteranwritingservices.com
www.facebook.com/believinginhorses
www.twitter.com/believeinhorses

www.jbmaxpublishing.com

Also Available from JB Max:

First, the move to Maryland. Then Dad's deployment to Afghanistan. Sadie is in trouble. Then she gets Lucky, a new young horse who proves to be a handful. But that's just the beginning. Together they encounter horse thieves, Maryland storms,and unwanted horses destined for auction and uncertain futures. Sadie makes it her personal mission to save them. Along the way she meets other people who are dedicated to rescuing horses. She also learns that some people in the horse industry are driven by greed.

Jenny and Jason are going on an adventure. With ever mounting excitement that they will soon be on the backs of their favorite horses, they learn about brushes, tack, safety rules, and that no two horses are alike. The colorful and entertaining cast of characters guides Jenny, Jason, and the reader through the world of horses. Vivid illustrations bring the book alive, and the prominent element is the joy and bond that exists between horse and human. Of course, no day at the barn is complete without a few unexpected events. Will Jenny be able to handle the spirited Amaretta? Will Jason overcome his pre-ride jitters?

Available from Veda Readers:

Teacher's Tack for Believing In Horses (Veda Readers, March 2012), provides educators lesson plans, discussion activities, and fun learning opportunities for a wide variety of ages and reading levels. Developed by Edward Ormond (AKA "EdUCator"), this 78-page comprehensive guide will make any teacher's job easier.

www.believinginhorses.com/veda_readers